C000262882

# A Time of Love,
# A Time of War

*By the same author*

The Homosaur
Child of Vodyanoi
(The Nightmare Man)
Genesis II
Beneath Us the Stars
Enduring Passions
The Tears of Autumn

*Under John Bedford*

Moment in Time
Operation Trigeminal
The Generals Died Together
The Titron Madness
The Nemesis Concerto

*BBC TV Production*

The Nightmare Man

# A Time of Love, A Time of War

DAVID WILTSHIRE

ROBERT HALE · LONDON

First published in Great Britain 2010

ISBN 978-0-7090-9016-8

Robert Hale Limited
Clerkenwell House
Clerkenwell Green
London EC1R 0HT

www.halebooks.com



2 4 6 8 10 9 7 5 3 1

Typeset in 10/13pt Palatino
by Derek Doyle & Associates, Shaw Heath
Printed in Great Britain by the MPG Books Group, Bodmin and King's Lynn

*For Olivia*

*LOVE - There is no instinct like that of the heart.*

Lord Byron

*WAR – Organized murder and nothing else.*

Private Harry Patch

# AUTHOR'S NOTE

The Second World War has now been over for sixty-five years, but continues to fascinate because for many, despite all the deprivation and sacrifice, it was the last time that Britain was truly Great – and happy: this happy breed of Shakespeare. It was, paradoxically, a gentler, simpler time.

This then is the enduring interest of the war years – a period of momentous events in which ordinary people played such a large part – and of always present danger, the uncertainty of life and death.

And for the survivors of the generation who lived through it, there is nostalgia for the days of their youth, and the memory of love affairs that blossomed far from home.

But for some, their fate was to remain forever 'young'.

Our story starts in 1943, over halfway through the war, as the tide is beginning to turn for the Allies.

# CHAPTER ONE

Walter Raus was freezing to death despite the greatcoat worn over his combat uniform, two pairs of gloves, a scarf wrapped around his neck and tucked in over his chest, and another over his head and ears, beneath his helmet.

His face was drawn, grey, showing the stubble of several days' growth. His lips were dry and chapped by the icy wind, from which he was sheltering behind the steel hulk of his tank, the snow swirling around the sides in the early morning dawn.

His crew were struggling with an oil burner set in a hole blown out of the iron-hard ground by explosives, trying to brew a pot of *ersatz* coffee.

They had been fighting and falling back for days now, first in the paralysing, biting frost and now in the blinding whiteness of the blizzard.

They had been attacked all the way by marauding bands of Cossacks equipped with white camouflage smocks and riding small amazingly tough horses. They came out of nowhere, striking hard at the marching columns of exhausted infantry, then disappearing back into the white wilderness.

He remembered their summer advance, across the terrifying emptiness of the open spaces of Russia, a vastness like an ocean, where you could pass a day without ever encountering another human being, let alone an enemy soldier.

He remembered the intense heat then, and the great columns of dust that had choked throats, blinded eyes despite goggles and neckerchiefs, and got into the engines as they advanced across the sun-baked steppes.

Even at that time, in the joy and camaraderie of their success, he and his brother officers had had doubts about their operational targets, ordered by Hitler, and had worried about the problems of resupply over thousands of kilometres of thinly held territory.

It was the first time he had entertained thoughts about the Führer's wisdom.

He had been a member of the Nazi Party since he had left the Hitler Youth Movement and gone into the army. When he was a boy he'd watched his father struggle to feed his family, working nights and weekends as a security porter, his days as a lawyer. In the end it had killed him – a man who had faithfully served his country in the war, winning a Knight's Cross for gallantry at Verdun.

No, Walter had eagerly embraced the Nazi Party for what it had done for his country.

And of course, when the Führer had launched his attack in the West, and it was all over in such a short, unbelievable time, and the French had been forced to surrender using the same railway carriage in which Germany had had to sign the Armistice in 1918, well, his admiration for his Führer knew no bounds.

But the great crusade against Bolshevism in the East had faltered after reaching the outskirts of Moscow and Leningrad.

It had become a struggle of the utmost ferocity, with immense loss of life.

Now they were retreating in order to regroup.

Walter Raus found his small flask of schnapps and took one sip. They had just heard of the fate of the Sixth Army at Stalingrad. It was unbelievable. For the second time a little bead of doubt formed in his mind.

As he put the flask back his hand touched a leather folder. He took it out and opened it, looking at the photograph of his wife, Inge, and himself on their wedding day.

Was it only a year ago? It seemed like a lifetime away.

He let his mind drift back. It had been a gloriously warm spring day; he tried desperately to remember that warmth, to feel the sun on his face. . . .

All the leaves on the linden trees had been fresh and green as he had waited in his dress uniform outside the beautiful baroque church in Erlangen, sporting his new rank of obersturmführer in a SS Panzer Grenadier regiment. In his hand he had held a signed copy of the Führer's *Mein Kampf*, given to all members of the party on their marriage.

He had gone into the cool interior of the church with his best man, Karl Eldfeld, a pilot in the Luftwaffe, who was now a prisoner in England. Walter had taken off his cap to reveal his blond hair, shining in a beam of light coming through a high church window, contrasting with the blackness of his uniform.

Later, after the ceremony, when Inge had lifted her veil, his joy had been complete.

She was so beautiful he still couldn't believe his luck that she was in love with him.

Her face was perfectly proportioned, her small nose set between two brown eyes. Her dark hair was cut short; the braids from her time in the League gone in favour of hygiene because she was a nurse in Berlin, a fact that worried him sick now that it was being bombed by the English and Americans.

They had been surrounded by their families, though his brother was not able to be there as he was serving on a U-boat somewhere in the Atlantic. They had used horses and four-wheeled carts decorated with wild flowers to go into the woods, which were alive and fresh with the spring.

Trout had been cooked over a fire; the guests had eaten them sitting on felled tree-trunks.

They had danced to a Bavarian country band and sung traditional songs.

Later, they had repaired to a local hotel where a three-piece orchestra had played tunes from films and shows. They had waltzed to the music from the film *Gone With the Wind*, one of Inge's favourites. They, as many, had seen illicit copies shown in private viewings. It was even rumoured in certain SS circles that the Führer had enjoyed it accompanied by Eva Braun.

With his new wife blushing furiously they had been clapped as they ascended the hotel's main staircase to their bedroom.

They had known each other nearly all their lives. Her father was a doctor, and had been in the same fencing club at university in Bamberg as his father.

But now Inge had looked for the first time upon her young husband without his black uniform, naked as the day he was born.

As a nurse she was well acquainted with the human male body, but even she was stirred by the sight of his strong perfect physique.

And he was all hers.

He lifted the sheet and slid into the bed beside her, their naked bodies touching for the very first time.

At last she was about to fulfil the promise she had made as a member of the League of German Maidens.

The summons, 'The Führer Needs You,' had greatly moved Inge, as it had most females of her generation.

The way in which women could really take part in the Thousand-Year Reich, was to be one of the guiding principles of families: that women should support their husbands and produce the children who were needed to become the future soldiers and workers of the Fatherland. Inge remembered being in her spotless uniform in the huge crowd to greet their 'Saviour' at Nuremberg, and the singing of the anthem *Die Fahne Hoch* – Raise High the Flag. She had taken part in swearing an oath of undying loyalty to their Führer.

The only time she had rebelled, if you could call it that, was when it came to her compulsory year of work, either on the land or in domestic service. With the influence of her father she had started training in a Berlin hospital as a nurse. She would continue until she had a baby for the Führer.

But the honeymoon had been short-lived. Two days later he had been ordered back to the front: the Russians had opened their expected offensive earlier than Intelligence had estimated.

Inge had come with him on the train to Berlin, then she had stood on the platform of the Friedrichstrasse station, looking up at him as crowds of troops formed up in orderly lines to board for their long journey east.

It broke his heart to leave her so quickly.

'I shall write tonight. Take care, my husband. . . .' She smiled coyly 'of two nights. I love you with all my heart.'

Whistles blew, boots stamped on the flagstones as some men ran to board.

He'd barely raised his hand to his lips and then blown a kiss to her when the awful wailing of the air-raid sirens started up.

People began running for the shelters as the train jerked into motion.

Inge walked to keep up with him as the carriage gathered speed, until eventually she had to stop.

As he drew further away he had tried to indicate that she should run for the shelter, but she was still there, a picture of steadfast German beauty, hand raised in farewell as they rounded a bend and she was lost from view.

Outside the station the night sky over the city was lit by searchlights. Above the still wailing sirens he could hear the crump of bombs.

The RAF was mounting a big raid.

Suddenly the flak tower over by the zoo opened up with a terrific barrage of 88mm fire as a radar-guided master light found an aircraft and all the slave searchlights rushed across the sky and covered it.

The train ground to a violent halt in a deep cutting, waiting for the raid to finish.

When their journey was resumed, and all the way back to the front, Walter Raus had never stopped worrying about Inge until he received a letter some three weeks later. He had written back straight away, pleading with her to leave Berlin for the country, but he knew she would always put her duty first.

As did he.

An NCO handed him a mug of steaming black liquid, bringing him back to the present.

'There we are, sir – you'd better hurry.'

Walter knew what the man meant. In these temperatures it would be frozen solid in five minutes.

All the same, he was careful when he put his lips to the metal; one could easily tear the skin off in this severe, sub-zero weather.

When he'd finished the coffee he stood, walked a little way away, and began the intricate job of having a pee without endangering his manhood.

Somewhere whistles began to blow. The break was over. As the men climbed back on to the tanks and trucks, other crew members pulled clear the trays of burning oil that had kept the engines from freezing up. With a roar the Panzer IIIs burst into life.

The great convoy was on the move again; many of the tanks and self-propelled guns and half-tracks were towing the lighter vehicles, the Kubbelwagons and other staff cars that had succumbed to the inhospitable environment.

In a few weeks the road would be metres deep in mud as the icy weather relinquished its grip with the coming of spring.

Walter looked to his left in the growing light. Far into the distance the white landscape was covered with dark smudges beginning to be covered with the fresh fall of snow, others moving piteously, like damaged ants.

Bodies.

They had repulsed the Russian attack less than an hour ago.

Hundreds of Soviets lay out there, their riderless horses galloping towards a frozen river in the far distance.

For a while the German soldiers would be disengaged from the regular Russian army, but what all the men feared most was a sudden ambush from the partisan terrorists.

And their atrocities.

# CHAPTER TWO

The American had run for miles along the wide sweep of the bay, right to the end of the beach, then along the banks of the Scarborough River before ending up once again at the ocean's edge.

His two dogs panted heavily as they milled around his feet before dropping to the ground.

The pink tongue of Blackie, the Labrador retriever, lolled out of his mouth, frothing saliva dripping on to the fine sand. 'Skipper', the grizzled brown-and-white Jack Russell terrier, was flat on his stomach, paws sticking out, his muscled body pumping like a little engine.

But John Fairfax's breathing was regular, and almost normal. After the preceding months, that was not surprising. At twenty-three he knew he would never be fitter, however long he lived. He gave a humourless chuckle – and that might not be very much longer.

He looked around. The nearest people he could see were tiny figures miles away, near the pier.

He let the small rucksack he was carrying slip to the sand by his feet, and pulled off his sweatshirt.

Naked, John Fairfax ran for the roaring surf, the dogs following. But as he splashed through the shallows, Skipper halted, barking furiously at his retreating back. Blackie managed a few waves, got to the point of swimming, head sticking up in the air as each breaking wave hissed past, then turned for terra firma as his master dived through a big one into deeper water and disappeared.

Despite the fine August weather, the bubbling green water of the Atlantic as it closed over his head was cold and invigorating.

He'd swum off the coast of Maine from boyhood. With strong strokes he cut through the foaming water in a fast crawl, going straight out for a quarter of a mile, then back again.

He emerged from the sea and ran, with the dogs jumping joyously around him, to his rucksack, got out a towel and started briskly drying himself, fending off the attention of the dogs with their sharp claws as he did so.

With his clothes back on he sat down and fished out his packet of Chesterfields, shook one free, and lit up. Skipper came and sat down on one side of him, followed quickly by Blackie on the other.

He watched as the fiery red ball that was the sun rising out of the waves, turning the cold green ocean to a warm purple, then at last a sparkling blue.

He breathed out smoke, and wondered. Would they be going in that direction – to Europe? Or, he half-turned and looked behind him across the fields in the direction of the railroad and West Scarborough and the still leaden sky of the departing night, that way, towards – Japan.

None of them knew. His body was iron hard, honed by months of intense physical training and route marches in all weathers with packs weighing anything up to half his body weight, running up hills and mountains again and again and again.

Coach Houseman at the high school would have been proud of him.

There had been less demanding lighter moments, if you could call them that. On the assault course he'd slipped and ended up face down in the mud.

In swift succession, his following platoon had delighted in using him as a jump-off for the ten-foot wall before them, putting a boot on to his back every time he tried to rise from the mire, plunging his face back into the mud.

But it was high jinks; there was no real malice. The men liked and respected their young second lieutenant.

Already they knew he would not ask them to do anything he wasn't prepared to do himself.

Last of all had come the jump training. Now he was a second lieutenant in a parachute regiment, part of the 101st Airborne Division the 'Screaming Eagles', and it was the day he had to set off, back to Camp Breckinridge. He knew the entire division would then transfer to Fort Bragg in North Carolina, a staging area, preparatory to shipping overseas.

But where?

To fight Adolf, or Hirohito?

Nobody knew, but they would find out once the trains started rolling on their long journey. If they went north, to New York, their destination would be England or Europe and the Mediterranean; if they went west, to California, then it would be the Pacific.

It was August 1943, and he had just two hours left before he began his journey back to his unit.

He flicked the stub away and stood up. It was time to go. The dogs bounced around and barked as he slung his rucksack over his shoulders and settled into an easy lope back along the sand towards his car.

He passed the pier where it seemed like only yesterday that he and all the gang had attended a Rudy Vallée concert. He turned up a side road and waved to the milkman in his cap and blue-and-white striped apron, who was delivering quarts of milk and cream to the white clapboard houses.

As soon as he opened the rear door of the parked Ford, Blackie leapt in, followed by Skipper. He got behind the wheel and closed the door. Twenty minutes later he turned on to a rising track that led through pine trees, coming out into a meadow full of flowers and long grass that gave way to the lawns of the rambling colonial-style house in which he had grown up. He parked the brake, let the dogs out, and walked round to the back of the house.

He could see that breakfast had been set on a table on the terrace. He stopped to pour himself a glass of freshly squeezed orange juice, just as his mother appeared with Louise their help, who was carrying a tray.

'Darling.' His mother looked worried. 'You're going to be late, and I do want you to have a good breakfast.'

He gave her a quick kiss on the forehead. 'Won't take me five – no, make that three minutes – to shower.'

With that he ran into the house, traversing the wood-beamed family room with the huge wide windows through which could be seen the ocean and a low rocky headland. Foaming waves showed where craggy boulders marked the edge of the blue sea. Rising above the water was the green of the densely packed Eastern White Pines.

He took the stairs two at a time and burst into his room. Its walls were decorated with college pennants; baseball and football trophies were scattered about on bookshelves.

Hurriedly he stripped and dashed for the shower.

He was nearly as good as his word. He did not stop to dress but pulled on his shorts and pushed his feet into his canvas shoes before wrapping himself in his robe. He was still tying the belt as he ran down the stairs and out on to the terrace.

His mother was already seated, nursing her coffee cup in two hands and looking pensive. He kissed her cheek, and felt his senses assailed by everything that was his mother: the taste of soap from her freshly washed skin, and the hint of her lavender perfume.

She covered his hand on her shoulder with one of her own, patting it.

He loved his mother, was proud of her looks, with her tall, willowy figure, clear blue eyes, high cheekbones and regular small teeth – his father always joked that these were what he'd noticed first about her, earning for himself his wife's raised eyebrow and mock look of pained disdain. His father was a dentist with an office in Boston.

As he settled into his chair and reached for the first of several Belgian waffles, he was aware that his mother was watching him intently.

There was an unfamiliar sadness about her.

He paused, smiling.

'Don't worry mother, I'll be all right. Granddad was OK, it runs in the Fairfax blood.'

The fact that Charlie Fairfax had been a doughboy in the last war, and had come home after surviving Belleau Wood did nothing to relieve Eleanor Fairfax of the awful worry that her son – her *only* son, would be in harm's way in the defence of his country.

She'd seen the news footage at the movies of the bitter fighting in the Pacific, and of the returning wounded, and it took all her self-restraint for her to act normally; but she couldn't stop tiny tears forming in the corners of her eyes. She thought, had ever a mother in her *right* mind – not like the Nazis or the Japanese women – not been terrified of her own flesh and blood going off to war?

She looked at her beautiful boy with his dark hair, clear blue eyes and infectious smile, then got control of herself again, but she couldn't help saying: 'Fairfax luck didn't work out too well in the Revolutionary War, or the Civil one for that matter.'

He grinned. It was true that one Jack Fairfax had died during the former, fighting, it had to be said, on the Loyalists' side, and one Obadiah Fairfax had been wounded at Gettysburg with the 20$^{th}$ Maine; he had succumbed to his wounds two weeks later.

'Well now, Mom, old Obadiah would have survived with today's surgery.'

He took a mouthful of waffle before adding, 'Anyway, don't be so gloomy, you're as bad as Betty.'

Betty was his girlfriend, had been since they'd met at college. Betty was blonde and wore her thick shining hair cut in a bob; her wide blue eyes brimmed with life and confidence, and she had a love of the open air that matched his own.

There had never been a formal announcement, just a sort of unspoken understanding that they were 'together'.

Betty had been a bit weepy last night in his drophead Studebaker. Parked on the top of a hill, they'd kissed and petted – it had been a long time since they had last been together, almost four months.

The radio had been on low with the soft voices of a crooner and a female vocalist fronting the Guy Lombardo Orchestra.

Betty Walsh had been conscious of the strength and rock hardness of his body. He had always been fit, but now he exuded an animal strength that frankly had left her breathless, both excited and a little fearful, suddenly aware of her vulnerability. But there was no one as gentle as John Fairfax, though he was *changed*, there was no doubt about that.

He was more thoughtful, quieter. When they'd been eating at a clam shack after walking hand in hand along the shore, she'd found that he kept sinking into silences.

Before he'd gone to the army he would have been talking away to her, wisecracking.

Sadly, she had realized that the army had taken the light-hearted boyfriend of her youth and turned him into a man.

He'd stirred, knew that the moment he had been worrying about had arrived.

'Darling, when I come back I'd like to think you'll be waiting for me.'

He'd looked pleadingly at her. 'But' – he paused again before saying with a rush – 'there's something inside of me that tells me I should be, well, *unattached* – until this is all over.'

Quickly he'd tried to put it another way. 'I don't want to burden you with extra worry.'

She'd looked down into her lap.

'So you don't want to get engaged?'

John Fairfax had felt very unhappy, but at last he managed to say, 'None of us knows what the future holds. I'm just saying we should put our lives on hold until this is all over.'

She'd continued to look down into her lap.

'I think I understand.' Her voice was very quiet.

He came back to the present as his mother poured some more coffee.

They ate in silence for a few moments, until his mother saw him checking his watch.

'What time is the cab expected, John?'

'I've got an hour, Mom.'

'Is Betty going to see you off?'

He shook his head. 'She's joining the Red Cross, by the way, she may go overseas as well.'

Eleanor Fairfax raised an eyebrow.

'Well, good for her. I *like* that girl.'

She paused, her pearls tinkling against her saucer as she leant forward to reach for the cream jug.

'Did you two make any plans last night?'

Wearily he nodded his head.

'Yes mother – not to do anything rash.'

He drained the last of his coffee.

'It doesn't seem the right moment to be planning the future.'

He was sorry as soon as he said it, it sounded so doom-laden.

But he needn't have worried. His mother had settled back into her New England reserve, which frowned upon any overt show of emotion.

He stood up.

'Time to get changed.'

When he came down the stairs with his canvas bag he was in his uniform, the coveted parachute wings on show.

He dropped his bag by the already open front door through which the warm sunshine came flooding in across the wooden floor. Outside the insects buzzed in the flowerbeds around the gravel drive.

In the room to his left was the family piano, a baby grand, which his mother played so beautifully. He had many happy memories of the family gathered around it at Thanksgiving and Christmas, singing along as she played anything from 'Swanee River' and 'John Brown's Body', to songs from the latest shows.

He had been a boy soprano in the choir of their white clapboarded church, which had been built in 1793, but one Thanksgiving, with early snow a foot deep outside, his voice had broken with disastrous results, right in the middle of a solo.

He had nearly died of embarrassment.

Then there had been his father, standing with his back to the fire, always giving a little Thanksgiving address to the family, usually on the lines of: 'America – the greatest country of them all'. A land of opportunity where there were no artificial barriers to prevent a hard-working man from fulfilling his potential, rising to any height he wanted, unlike in the old world of birth, class, and custom.

He remembered him wagging his finger as he had added that it was that which had finally hauled the country out of the great depression.

His mother appeared with a large-brimmed hat and gloves, and laid them on a side table. She was obviously going to do some gardening. His father had said goodbye the night before, and had now gone back to Boston for the week.

'My my, how handsome you look, and so strong.'

John Fairfax winced.

'Might you not be a little bit biased, Mom?'

'Of course, darling, but that doesn't stop it being true.'

There was a crunching of tyres on the gravel drive as 'Pete's Cabs' drew up at the door.

Pete himself got out, an aged rotund man with a small moustache.

He touched the peak of his cap to the lady of the house.

'Good morning, Mrs Fairfax.' He turned his attention to John.

'Wow, you've changed a lot, young fellow.'

He opened the wood-panelled door of the brake, grabbed John Fairfax's bag and heaved it on to the back seat. That done, Pete touched his cap again, and got back behind the wheel, realizing that this was a private moment for the young soldier, whom he had known since he was knee-high to a grasshopper, and his mother.

John faced Eleanor, glad that Pete was a little early and that everything was happening quickly. It would make it easier to leave.

'Well, goodbye Mom, I'll write as soon as I can.'

He wrapped his arms around her slim body, feeling the fine bones of her ribs as he gave her a hug. They hung on for several seconds, Eleanor Fairfax patting his back, before he let her go, kissed her on the cheek, and dropped into the front seat beside Pete.

He shut the door. Suddenly, as the engine started up, his mother ducked her head in through the window and kissed him once again on the forehead.

As the car pulled away he waved, kept waving, watching her as the car turned through the trees until her slim figure was lost from view.

At the railroad station he hauled his bag from the back. Pete wouldn't take any money, said it was on him, and 'Give-em-hell – son.'

The train was on time, the locomotive of the Maine Central rumbled past where he stood to come to a halt with a squeal of brakes.

As the black attendants let down the steps young men in uniform said passionate farewells to their girlfriends. He guessed it was a scene being repeated all over the nation as its youth prepared to go to war.

His father had been an isolationist, deeply committed to keeping America out of the war in Europe. The Japanese attack on Pearl Harbor had completely wrong-footed him, especially as Herr Hitler had immediately declared war on the US.

He'd pleaded with John to finish his law studies at Harvard but, like all his friends, he'd been outraged by the unprovoked assault and loss of American lives.

The sight of the *Arizona* blazing in the water and the lists of dead and missing had left him numb with shock, then he was filled with an anger the like of which he'd never experienced before in his life.

It *demanded* he do something. Like hundreds of thousands of his fellow Americans he hadn't, *couldn't* wait for the draft.

Suddenly the engine gave a long low blast on its klaxon and shouts of 'all aboard' echoed down the station.

Slowly the extra-long wartime train began to move.

In the following hour he watched the clean little towns with their white church spires set in the green fields and woods of New England slip by. In truth he was tense with anticipation as to what the future held; one moment he was excited with all the bursting energy and sense of invincibility of the young, the next this was replaced with a sinking feeling in the pit of his stomach.

He was anxious on many counts, not least, would he perform well? Or would he disgrace the family and his country, and worst of all, let down the men under his command?

It didn't bear thinking about.

The days passed in a welter of routine: drill, runs with full packs, more weapon training, broken only by visits to the camp movie house, and calls – collect – to home, and to Betty.

But the tension was racking up, day on day until, three weeks later, on a bright sunny morning, the movement orders came through at last.

The excitement was tangible; you could almost taste it in the air.

In the headquarters company office all was a pandemonium of telephone bells, clacking typewriters and men coming and going with snappy salutes and message sheets.

John Fairfax returned a salute from a soldier as he descended the steps of the hut and made for his platoon, which was housed in tents.

Next day the division assembled, company upon company, battalion upon battalion, regiment upon regiment. With pennants and colours heading the formations, they marched past a saluting base and on to the twenty trains needed to take the 14,000 men of the 101st Airborne Division – the Screaming Eagles – off to war.

A band played 'Over There.'

It was a stunning sight; these were America's finest in overwhelming numbers, and it left them all feeling intensely proud.

They were the product of the greatest gamble the US Army had ever made: an élite airborne force, capable, as the press had dubbed it, of 'Vertical Invasion'. Now they were on their way to find out whether the gamble of diverting men and resources would pay off.

They were superbly fit, highly trained and prepared for anything the enemy could throw at them.

Red Cross girls handed out doughnuts and coffee, and waved and cried as the grossly overloaded trains pulled out of the station yard, and headed *north*, towards New York.

The mystery was over.

As he settled into his seat, having checked that his boys were OK, John Fairfax could only think of old Charlie Fairfax in 1917. Had he felt the same mixture of excitement and pride, mixed with such gut-churning fear at what lay ahead? Trained as they were to immense standards of fitness and imbued with military skills, there was still no substitute for experience. Those whom he had met who had been there were a race apart.

They eventually reached Camp Shanks thirty miles north of New York on the Hudson River. There the medics really took over. John was given shots for so many things that his arms felt leaden and weak.

The men were also made to take off their 'airborne' flashes, so that spies in New York would not be able to report the arrival of a crack division shipping out to England to spearhead an invasion of 'Fortress Europe'.

Since it was the Japanese who had actually attacked the United

States, it was reckoned that the Axis powers would guess that Japan was the nation against whom the growing military and industrial might of the nation would first be pitted.

Leave passes were given for New York, and he spent a pleasant day just walking through Central Park, then going to the movies. He saw *Mrs Miniver* with Greer Garson and Walter Pidgeon – a story of an English woman and her civilian husband, going in his little weekend boat to rescue British troops off the beaches of Dunkirk, ordinary people doing extraordinary, heroic things.

The next morning the company marched down to the docks, where they were jammed on to Hudson River ferries and carried across to piers where more hot coffee and doughnuts were distributed by more Red Cross girls. A lump came into John Fairfax's throat at the thought of Betty in her uniform.

Then, in a near endless snaking column, shouldering their heavy duffel bags and weapons, they hauled themselves up a gangway into an old Cunard cruise ship, now under the command of the British Navy. As they stepped on to the deck they shouted out their names to a checker, who marked them off a list, and descended below, guided by crewmen until they reached their allotted space below the waterline.

It took all day for the 5,000 men assigned to their ship to crowd into an old liner built to carry 1,000 passengers. Each bunk was to be used in eight-hour shifts by three different men.

John Fairfax made sure his men were in the right place, had their lifejackets issued, which they had to wear at all times when they were at sea, apart from when they were in their bunks, then returned to the deck, as did most men, for the departure.

He leant on the rails, watching the longshoremen make the ship ready for sea, hauling down the gangways and casting off hawsers, as tugs nudged and hauled the ship away from the quay. Waving New Yorkers gathered to see them off as bands played the stirring marches of Sousa, before ending with the *Star Spangled Banner*.

Over the past year the citizens had seen many a ship taking their boys off to war, but it was always a deeply moving experience.

For a finale a police pipe band started playing *Amazing Grace*.

For a while a relative silence descended over the thousands of people, troops and civilians alike, the plaintive tone of the pipes adding to the soul-searching depth of the old Olney hymn. John Fairfax had sung it since he was a choirboy.

He wondered whether, when he reached England, he'd be able to get to the small town where it had probably been written. Then, as clear water began to show between them and land, the band started playing *Auld Lang Syne*.

Twenty minutes later, to the accompaniment of the whooping sirens of the tugs as they relinquished their grip on their charge, answered by blasts from the funnel of the old ship, they got under way, and were soon slipping quietly past the Statue of Liberty, heading for the open sea. Most of the men had never been abroad before, including John Fairfax if you didn't count Canada.

Only the hiss of the sea beneath the prow, and the harsh cries of the wheeling seagulls accompanied the thoughts of those on deck: thoughts of a home they might never see again.

As Sandy Hook receded into the dusk the ship's engines thumped slowly as she made her way in a gathering mist to join a convoy forming off Long Island.

The decks began to empty, no smoking was allowed on deck as a total blackout came into effect.

With his now obligatory lifejacket on, John Fairfax took a last stroll to the stern and looked down at the white wake that pointed to an already invisible America; an America wherein lived all the loved ones he wanted to protect – and come home to.

He guessed that if he made it back, for him nothing would be the same again.

It was an end to childhood, an end to innocence.

# CHAPTER THREE

In the dawn, all over East Anglia, above the quaint old towns and thousand-year-old cathedrals the planes appeared. They came out of the low scudding clouds, streaming home from the great air battle that had raged that night over the Third Reich.

The faster twin-engined Mosquitoes came first, the four-engined Lancasters last.

On the airfield they were watched through binoculars by men in RAF raincoats, standing on control tower roofs and from the top of ambulances and crash tenders. Civilians astride bikes in the rain-soaked lanes gazed skywards, and on tractors in the sodden fields farmworkers too looked up. Others stood in shop and cottage doorways, or leaned out of bedroom windows in the villages.

All eyes followed the droning aircraft. Most people felt themselves to be 'experts' now, after many months of experience, regarding the health or otherwise of an engine, and would search for the sight of any damage to the fuselage or tailplane, or of a feathered prop. All had been praying for the safe return of the men inside them.

Sometimes there were three or four or more planes together, at other times a lone one, limping on three engines and leaving a thin trail of black, oily smoke, perhaps bringing back dead and dying men on board; often there was a 4,000 pound bomb still clearly visible, jammed in the bay.

Very often, when their prayers went unanswered, there would come a heart-stopping boom, echoing across the land, and in the distance a pall of black smoke would rise above the trees.

It was over for another night.

For some it was over for ever.

*

The young flight lieutenant was upside down, bare feet blackened with soot and water pressed hard against the mess ceiling, accompanied by catcalls, jeers and cheers when he first laid eyes on her, standing in the doorway. Even from the wrong way up she took his breath away.

It was his undoing. Concentration lost, the pile of furniture on which he was balancing buckled. He had a fleeting sensation of her horrified face, then he was crashing in a pile of wreckage and bouncing off the heavy dining table, knocking over several chaps, and sending their beer glasses flying. In the mêlée that followed he surfaced at last to find the doorway empty.

He looked desperately around. He couldn't see her anywhere, then he realized that a little knot of his fellow officers were paying no attention to the mayhem in the room.

He made his way over, pulling at the nearest undone jacket, sending its occupant spinning away to crash into an impromptu rugby scrum.

And there she was, talking to the station CO. She was petite, slim, with soft auburn hair falling in waves to the nape of her neck, dressed in a grey tweed skirt with a blue woollen jumper and a little row of pearls. She held her shoulders squarely.

She must have been looking out for him, because she turned her head, stared straight at him, her dark eyes bright and intelligent. They stayed like that for seconds. She saw a young fresh-faced boy with a shock of dark Brylcreemed hair brushed straight back with a parting on the left. He had a firm mouth and jaw, and grey eyes that seemed older than his years.

The station CO, suddenly aware that she was looking past his shoulder, turned and saw him.

'Ah, Flight Lieutenant Cochran, I might have known. Where is your jacket?'

It had been discarded at the start of his ascent up the wobbling tower of hastily stacked furniture, so he was showing his braces.

'Sorry sir. It got in the way.'

The CO lifted an eyebrow.

'And your shoes and socks?'

'Just doing a little ceiling walking, sir, to celebrate.'

'Hmm.' The CO nodded at the girl.

'There are ladies present, Cochran. Get properly dressed.'

But he wasn't listening. There was something about her, the way she stared levelly back at him. She was good-looking, but it was the strength of her face that held him, especially her dark eyes. They bore into him as her mouth lifted in a wry smile.

'What are you celebrating?'

To his surprise the voice had a soft Irish accent.

'We've just come off ops – stood down for a week. Letting off a bit of steam.'

There was another roar from the centre of the room, and a fire extinguisher started to squirt white foam over a bunch of navigators who were balancing full pint glasses on their heads. Glasses crashed to the floor, spilling their contents as cushions were picked up to protect faces. Somebody threw a chair.

The station commander put a protective arm around his charge and ushered the others in the group towards the door.

'I'm afraid we'd better leave. Would you like to see the hangars?'

Cochran watched as they went through the door, and wondered whether. . . .

She did. Just before she went out of sight she looked back at him over her shoulder.

Slap!

A wet towel taken from a mess steward hit him on the side of his face with such force that he staggered, and tripped over the wing commander's dog, a corgi, which immediately attacked his groin. A hand came down and helped him to his feet. It was Davey, his handlebar-moustached navigator.

'Come on, Skipper. Bloody dog, ought to drop it over Berlin – give old Goebbels a nip where it hurts – if he's got any balls at all.'

Robbie Cochran slapped him on the shoulder.

'Thanks Davey. Hang on, I'll be back in a minute.'

He found his battledress blouse where he'd thrown it, but there was no sign of his shoes and socks. He ran out, down the corridor, pulling the blouse on and trying to button it up, then wincing and hopping on one leg as he stubbed his toe.

Outside in the dark he made his way across the wet grass to the side of the first hangar.

Inside, several sleek aircraft were being worked on, men on mobile metal gantries were poring over the exposed engines, others were on the wings, bending into the cockpits.

He ducked under a wing, couldn't see the group.

'Something you want, sir?'

The leading aircraftman mechanic in overalls, covered in streaks of grease, looked at him in puzzlement.

'Yes, have you seen a visitor group?'

'The concert party? Over there, sir, looking at the propeller store.'

He could just see the backs of civilians crowded into a partitioned side area.

'Thanks.' He turned and stubbed his bare foot on a toolbox.

'Oh Jeez.'

Limping, he made off.

The LAC shook his head in disbelief.

Robbie came up to the group just as they started coming back out of a side area led by the group captain, whose eyes fell on Robbie. He stopped in his tracks and groaned.

'Not you again, Cochran.'

The group captain turned to the assembled civilians and rolled his eyes in a pained expression.

'Flight Lieutenant Cochran is one of our more colourful New Zealand pilots.'

The boys from the Dominions were less restrained than their British counterparts, especially when it came to authority.

Robbie had almost faced court martial for the dangerously low 'beating up' of airfields on his return, and for the blacking of the eyepieces of the officers' binoculars in the control tower, so that they had all looked like panda bears with big rings round their eyes. These officers had included the group captain, who continued with: 'Now, come this way; there will be food provided in the administration block.' The civilians all started to move.

As she passed him, her tongue pushed into her cheek.

'Very colourful.'

He swallowed, tried to speak, but nothing came out.

She chuckled. 'Lost your tongue, flight lieutenant, as well as your socks?'

He went bright red, blurted out: 'I wonder if you'd like to come for a drink?'

She raised one elegant eyebrow, seemed to be laughing at him.

'Of what?'

Wincing, he swallowed. 'Whatever you'd like.'

She glanced to check where the rest of the party were, to find they were nowhere in sight, except for a waiting corporal, who was still expectantly holding on to the blackout curtain. She looked back at him, biting her lip; then seemed to make up her mind and said: 'I'll meet you after the Saturday performance in the Bedford Corn Exchange, say about nine o'clock, in the front lobby?'

Without waiting for an answer she disappeared through the held-open curtain, which then dropped back, and she was gone.

He didn't go back to the mayhem in the mess, feeling suddenly out of it. Instead he lay on his bed, lit a cigarette, imagining her, especially those eyes, one moment quite intense, the next, soft and beguiling.

Maybe it was because she reminded him somehow of Kate, the girl whose bulging satchel he had sometimes carried, back home in New Zealand.

Kate, whose slim figure he had watched at a distance, streaking down the field playing hockey, or leaping high at netball. She too had an air of self possession – like this girl. But even at seventeen Kate had had to wear her uniform with white ankle socks like all of the girls at her school.

Because of his shyness nothing had ever happened, just a lot of intense talking, but he knew that, if the war hadn't come along, somewhere, sometime he would have plucked up courage to ask her out to the pictures.

Which made his impulsive behaviour tonight incredible.

Was it because he was older?

Was it the war?

Or was it something else?

On Saturday he bummed a ride in a three-tonner going to Bedford, conscious that all the British boys on board were bound for the station and from there on to home.

The lorry trundled down the main road, the A6. Having been the last one to climb aboard he had a view out through the back. In the distance, over the hedges, he could see mile upon mile of stacked ordnance: bombs for the US bases at Thurleigh, Podington, Chelveston and Kimbolton. The RAF attacked Nazi Germany by night, the US Eighth Air force attacked by day. Round the clock.

The truck turned into the cobbled forecourt of a redbrick Victorian station, and drew to a halt. The driver came around and dropped the tailgate. Robbie jumped down, followed by the others who made straight for the arched covered entrance. A whistle sounded and the steady *chuff-chuff* of a steam engine increased in tempo.

The driver raised the tailgate, jammed in the retaining pins, saluted and made for his open cab door.

Robbie went to him as he put his foot up on to the running board. 'Which way is it to the town centre and the Corn Exchange?'

Leaving one arm resting on the open door, the driver pointed.

'Straight up there, sir.'

In the gathering gloom Robbie walked up a street of small shops, shabby after more than four years of war. They got bigger until, after passing a cinema, he reached a grammar school. The town was busy with pedestrians and cyclists ringing their bells. Little groups of servicemen were wandering aimlessly around, mostly American Army Air Force, and RAF personnel.

He found a church with a tall steeple, opposite which stood a large building, which turned out to be the Corn Exchange.

Inside, the spacious hall was already filling up. He squeezed into a seat at the back, not wanting her to see him. Puzzled, he saw the stage was set up for a large orchestra. He was disappointed that he couldn't find her anywhere as the musicians started to tune up. Had she been misleading him all along? A tail-coated conductor appeared and the audience started to clap.

He had no option but to sit back as the concert began. At least he knew the first piece from schooldays. When the overture was finished the conductor briefly bowed to the applause and left the stage. Two men in brown coats came on and wheeled the grand piano from the side to the centre of the platform. They locked the wheels, placed the stool in position and raised the lid.

The orchestra finished retuning and silence descended once more. Depressed, he was wondering how long he would have to sit there before he could get away, when the side door opened and, escorted by the conductor, a slim young woman in a plain black cocktail dress entered. For several seconds he couldn't take in what his eyes were telling him – that it was *her*.

She reached the piano, placed a hand on it as she acknowledged the applause, then sat on the stool and adjusted it. When she was ready she nodded at the conductor, who brought his baton down and started the orchestra.

Robbie sat transfixed as her hands raced over the keyboard, sometimes caressing the keys, at others powering down with a strength that belied her slim figure. The light reflected off a slide in her hair as she moved her head with the effort and emotion of the music. It was Greig's Piano Concerto.

Later, when the final chords died away the audience burst into prolonged applause. After she had acknowledged them and then indicated the orchestra, she left accompanied by the conductor. She came back twice more, received a bunch of home-grown flowers, and that was that.

Robbie had never taken his eyes off her from the moment she appeared to the last sight of her as she went out through the door, the light making her slender bare arms quite white against the black of her dress. The orchestra began to rise to their feet. It was the interval.

Nervously he hung around in the lobby as everybody returned to their seats for the second part of the concert. It was empty when suddenly. . . .

'Hello.'

He whirled around.

If anything she was more beautiful, more radiant than he remembered; he didn't realize that it was because of the small amount of make-up she had on.

She was dressed in a camel-hair coat belted at the waist, with a high, wide collar such as had been in fashion in the thirties. On her head she wore a black beret with a red bobble; it matched the colour of her lips and was pulled down to one side. One hand was holding on to the straps of her shoulder bag and gas mask carrier.

Her eyes were bright, her face a little flushed.

Amazed, Robbie croaked: 'You came?'

Voice teasing, she said: 'Yes, of course. I said I would.'

He nodded in the direction of the auditorium.

'I had no idea, you were so – well, famous.'

For the first time she openly laughed.

'Don't be silly. I'm still a student; we get roped in when there are not enough soloists and players to go around.' She aped a posh voice. 'Got to keep up the nation's morale – there's a war on, don't you know?'

Briefly her face clouded. Strictly it wasn't her war really, she being Irish. But as a student on a scholarship at the music academy, she had become a Londoner, suffering the bombing raids and food shortages of the previous four years. Even so, it was still safer than being at home. . . .

Her thoughts were interrupted by his saying: 'I'm Robbie Cochran.'

He held out his hand.

She took it. 'Maddie Hayes.'

They shook, just the once; her hand was surprisingly firm.

When he didn't say anything more she looked at her watch, raised one eyebrow and said pointedly: 'That drink?'

Galvanized and embarrassed he exclaimed: 'Of course – sorry.'

He led the way, holding the door for her as they went out into the street. He was conscious of her closeness and a faint scent of something that made his senses reel.

'Shall we go to the Swan Hotel, is that where you are staying?'

She chuckled. 'The ministry doesn't pay for anything like that. We girls have been put up in a college dorm, and we go back to London tonight.'

Disappointed he muttered: 'I see. Right. Well it's just across the road.'

At the hotel the bar was smoke-filled and crowded. He found a corner with a ledge along the wall.

'What will you have?'

She began to undo her coat.

'I could do with a whisky with water, if they have one. Is that all right?'

'Of course.'

Surprised, he pushed his way to the counter. When he came back she had commandeered a stool and had taken off her coat.

'Phew, it's hot in here.'

He nodded, handed her the whisky.

'Tell me if you need more water.'

She took a sip. 'No, that's perfect.'

He took out his Woodbines and offered them to her. She took one. Robbie studied her closely as she leaned forward to the lighter he was holding, drawing in the smoke.

She sat back with a sigh.

'I needed that.'

He lit his own cigarette.

She sipped her drink, looked up at him over the rim of her glass.

'You're very brave, doing what you do. Must be frightening.'

Robbie frowned, shook his head.

'It takes guts to be in a sub, or the bloody infantry. I get a warm bed after I've done my bit.'

She could see he was embarrassed and changed the subject.

'Cochran? You're of Scottish descent then?'

He brightened. 'My grandparents were from Ayrshire.'

She beamed. 'I'm Irish, but I expect you guessed that.'

Robbie grinned ruefully. 'Yes.'

She told him about the scholarship, how she was studying piano under Sir Miles, whoever that was. Maddie talked without really hearing herself, still struggling with the madness that had made her accept his invitation. Seeing him again had not diminished it.

She took a gulp of her whisky to steady her nerves, conscious of what she was about to say.

'Why not come up to London. Tomorrow? I understand you've all got a few more days' leave, right? We could do something.' She tried to affect nonchalance, flicking her cigarette ash into a tray.

Robbie could hardly believe his ears.

'Yes.'

She put her head to one side, smiled. 'Yes – to what?'

'Yes to everything.'

Relieved, she just nodded, and said, as off-handedly as she could manage, despite the thumping in her chest, 'Good, I'll give you the address of a hotel I play at in the evening. I need the money.'

Maddie searched in her bag, found a piece of paper and a fountain pen and wrote down the address, hoping he couldn't see her slightly shaking hand.

He took it, put it in the top pocket of his battledress and rebuttoned the flap.

As if in reaction to what had just happened they talked about other things until she looked at her watch.

'Time to go, I'm afraid.'

Outside, in the dark street, lit only by the narrow strips of light coming from the masked headlights of buses and lorries, he asked her: 'Can I see you to the station?'

He was disappointed as he saw the dark outline of her head shake from side to side as she replied: 'No.'

She said nothing more.

There was a pause, which she suddenly ended.

'Bye bye, Robbie.'

With that she was gone, leaving him feeling deflated.

As the overcrowded train took her slowly back to London, stopping at every station, sometimes standing for ages at empty platforms, Maddie Hayes stared out of the window, seeing only the odd whisp of white steam in the blackness. But it was the reflection of her face she was really looking at, and questioning.

What had she done? She had always been so driven, so single-minded. To get where she was had meant years of hard work and practice: shutting herself in rehearsal rooms, going over passages of music hundreds of times, weeping, starting again, striving for perfection.

And now, in a moment of insanity she had . . . what?

Her face clouded.

At last the train steamed into a gloomily lit St Pancras station, over an hour and a half late.

As she came out on to the Euston Road she could see, in the east, searchlights flickering across the night sky. After a period of ever-decreasing German raids there had been markedly more activity in the last week.

But there was no noise of bombs or the anti-aircraft guns; just the silent beams of light glowing on the underside of the clouds.

# CHAPTER FOUR

For John Fairfax the voyage was ghastly. Fresh water was severely rationed, and the salt-water showers were ice cold. Everybody slept in their clothes, and when they were awake they crashed around in their life jackets and cartridge belts with canteens attached, constantly barging into each other in the gangways.

Many were seasick. The smell of puke and urine mingled with the odour of boiled fish slop being served from huge pots by the cooks.

On the second week at sea scabies broke out, thanks to fatigue uniforms only being able to be washed in cold seawater; this left them with rough edges that abraded their wearers' skin. The medics applied gentian violet to the irritated zones, which fluorescently stained all their clothing.

The overcrowded ship settled into a daily routine. When he could, John Fairfax walked the decks, looking at the huddles of men playing black jack, poker and craps, or watching other ships of the convoy, sometimes so scattered after a storm that they were on the horizon, at other times close enough for the men to shout at each other across the hissing foam-capped waves. Destroyers raced around their charges like collie dogs around sheep, sounding off their wailing klaxons and making smoke whenever there was a danger of U-boats.

Several men leaning over the rails reported seeing periscope wakes. He knew that there would be horrendous loss of life if they were torpedoed: men wouldn't last long in the cold, dark water of the North Atlantic. Such a disaster might affect the course of the war. Thankfully nothing ever came of any of these alarms, but it frightened the hell out of them all. Just when it seemed that they would be on the high seas forever, the cry 'Land ho!' came from the Tannoys.

Thousands of men tried to rush to the rails at once, causing the ship to list slightly.

It took some time for the landlubbers to see it: a low, dark line almost lost in a hazy grey horizon that was growing more indistinct with the failing light.

It was Ireland.

'Not very green, is it?' said Second Lieutenant John McCarthy, seeing the land of his ancestors for the very first time.

Many hours later they nosed up the Mersey to Liverpool in the pitch dark, broken only by the navigation lights of the tugs and the pilot's tender when it came alongside. The very effective blackout made them aware that they were, at last, in a combat zone.

Before the night was out they saw searchlights and flashes and heard explosions in the distance as a Luftwaffe raid on the city got under way. He swallowed. It was his first experience of real war and he shuddered at the thought of the death and destruction that was raining down on the citizens. They all stood in silence, watching.

By the time they started disembarking the dawn had come up; now the dockside was wreathed in a cordite-smelling fog, the aftermath of the night's onslaught.

It was a chastening welcome to England.

The train they boarded was dirty, small and so crowded that men were jammed into its compartments and side corridors, almost unable to move.

But nobody minded. It was heaven just to be off the old, sick tub of a boat they had been on.

The anti-blast netting stuck to the windows made it all but impossible to see out. Those who could see through the small lozenge-shaped areas left clear reported tired-looking groups of people on the raised railroad platforms, giving the 'V' for victory salute.

The train ground to a halt many times. Somebody dropped a window. A first lieutenant from the Mid West whistled as he took in the trim hedgerows and small fields, so unlike the vast spaces of his home state. 'It's really compact out there.'

'France is much the same,' said somebody.

The words hung in the air, because by now they all guessed that that was where they were going to end up.

They eventually arrived at a place called Hungerford, where they fell in on the station forecourt. It was an absolute pleasure to march the six miles to the area where they were to stay under canvas, scattered around a farm, behind an inn, and in the grounds of a manor house.

John Fairfax made sure his men were fixed up, then made his way to the manor house where he was billeted. On the way he passed a Norman church and a village green surrounded by thatched cottages with wisps of smoke curling from their chimneys, despite its being midsummer.

Although he had been expecting the 'oldness' of England, the sight and, more important, the smell of the old house was quite something; it seemed to be composed of dampness, log fires and centuries of dust.

In an oak-panelled room that looked like something out of a Sherlock Holmes movie he sat down with his brother officers at a long table laid with silver spoons and fine bone china. Even after the privations of the last few weeks he only needed a shower, albeit lukewarm, and he began to feel human again.

By a lucky fluke he had a room all to himself, probably because of its size – like a broom closet. But what a closet.

As he tucked in under a clean sheet he looked at the old gnarled beams and massive rafters. When he turned out the light it was pitch black. Only when his eyes had adjusted did he see the stars shining brightly through the quaint oriel-window.

Slowly he became aware of a low roar, like distant thunder, gradually swelling, growing into an intense noise that vibrated his travelling clock and other of the room's contents.

It was the sound of hundreds of aircraft, unseen in the night sky. There were shouts of alarm down the corridor, and a cry of 'air raid,' before wiser, older hands counselled.

'Forget it, that's the RAF going over to give the Krauts their nightly visit. Our boys do it in the daylight, giving them a hell of a shellacking – round the clock, it's called, softening them up.'

Fairfax took off his helmet and crawled back into his bed, listening until the noise slowly subsided, eventually fading to nothing.

What with their arrival in Liverpool, the long train journey down to Hungerford in Berkshire County and now this, he suddenly felt very homesick.

He wondered what Betty was doing just then, and his mother and father and sis.

Downstairs a radio was playing and a woman was softly singing the song Gene Kelly had crooned in the movie 'Cover Girl', which he'd seen in the camp theatre the night before they had entrained. 'Long Ago and Far Away.' That was what home seemed now.

He was still feeling sorry for himself when sleep overcame him in seconds.

The powers that be wasted no time in getting them back into physical shape. They ran and marched all over the gently rolling countryside, by mellow stone-built thatched cottages, past old inns with names like the White Hart and the Six Bells, across village greens, past Norman churches and down narrow lanes, sometimes meeting teams of vast horses called shires, which were used for ploughing. The locals told them they were descended from warhorses ridden by knights of old. The same locals listened, puzzled, when the squads went past chanting:

*They're just two things that we can't stand,*
*A bow-legged woman and a straight-legged man.*

He explained to a bemused vicar that 'Straight leg' was the paratroops' name for the rest of the army, who didn't need to remember to bend their legs on hitting the ground.

Back Stateside, they had always been billeted far from civilian centres, but here they were all mixed up with the villages and their inhabitants, who at first regarded them anxiously, but then warmly welcomed them. Companies were scattered on farms, or school playing fields, behind inns and on country estates.

Southern England was now becoming one vast army base with millions of men under arms. The Americans had been subjected to lectures on English customs and habits, and were told that although they could have a quiet pint in the local pubs they should treat them as if they were used by Ma and Pa, and should only hell-raise in the larger centres of Swindon and London on weekend passes.

John Fairfax found a little tumbledown place, extraordinarily called 'The Case is Altered'. The sign outside had a picture of a bewigged lawyer and a quill pen.

There, a couple of times a week, when they were not out on manoeuvres, he enjoyed a quiet pint of 'warm' English ale and played dominoes and other pub games, or sat in an atmosphere of peace and quiet, staring at the sawdust-covered floor, glad to be, for a moment, away from the shouting, noisy military life and the increasingly tense expectation of what was to come.

*

Their training increased in tempo and direction. It was obvious that they were being prepared for the invasion of France. John Fairfax led his men in street-fighting exercises, night operations, and the familiarization with German equipment, from weapons to booby traps, mines and communications.

On top of this they were again jumping regularly, testing their abilities in the cold, turbulent English skies, training to land avoiding the dangerous, cluttered terrain of hedgerows, telephone poles, stone walls, woods and lakes.

'Stand up, hook up,' shouted the jumpmaster in the C47 transport, then: 'Move to the door.'

John Fairfax stepped to the open hatch, through which freezing air was blasting in, remembering to keep his eyes on the horizon. Every time was a repeat of his first 'cherry' jump, the anxiety and thrill much the same. Now they were jumping with increasing amounts of equipment, sufficient to keep them self-sustained for several days after landing. There was even an equipment bag developed by the Limeys; it was attached to the leg by a cord and it hit the ground first.

On the green light he stepped forward. He was sucked out into the roar of engines and blasting wind, then he felt a blow to his chest as the chute deployed.

Afterwards came the same beautiful silence, with only a gentle sigh of the wind through his rigging. He looked down between his swaying feet, at the patchwork quilt of the English countryside. It was not unlike the pictures he'd seen of France.

New officers were coming in regularly now, the aim being to have two lieutenants per platoon; the top brass were anticipating, they all realized, heavier casualties than the ordinary footsloggers would sustain.

It also meant that at last he was given a six-day pass.

That night he wrote a letter, using a flashlight for illumination under the bedclothes as the power failed yet again, and it was so cold and damp.

Betty was now in the Red Cross.

He told her how much he missed her, that never a night passed without the thought of her and (daringly) of her sweet face and woman's figure. He decided he'd gone too far, staring at it for some time before scrubbing it out. Perhaps it was the realization among them all, that the big show couldn't be too far away, which was making him uncharacteristically poetic and daring; that, or was he over-compensating for feelings that weren't there?

He finished with a row of crosses to represent kisses, and felt guilty as hell.

His letters to his parents he had always kept light, describing those parts of England that he had so far managed to reach by local buses, deliberately not giving place names and concentrating mostly on architecture, especially the cathedrals and churches.

The people of the counties of Berkshire and Wiltshire had proved to be warm and friendly, and had often invited the men into their houses for tea or supper, but the CO and Eisenhower himself had warned the men that the locals could ill afford to share their meagre rations, and that they should politely refuse. However, some had taken to bringing stuff from the PX to help out, they were so glad to be in a real home.

He'd found that British houses were only heated by open fires and gas and electric appliances. Central heating was confined to public buildings.

He'd visited one of the terraced houses in Swindon on regimental business. When he'd stood in the room, hat respectfully off, he had been amazed at how tiny it was, at the tiled surround of the fireplace with trinkets on the mantelpiece, and three 'flying ducks' on the flowered wallpaper opposite.

He'd nearly tripped over an easy chair, which with its pair and a matching settee all in uncut moquette with large rounded arms nearly filled the living space. The white antimacassars and ashtrays on leather strips over the arms were often seen he had been told later.

This time he kept his letter short, only saying that he was excited about his leave, and that he was going to get away from it all and would write a much longer missive to tell them all about it next time.

He promised to take care and behave himself, and go to church, and added that he missed them very much, and the wide beaches and rocky coast of his beloved Maine.

Satisfied, he folded both the airmails but did not seal them, knowing they would have to be read by the censor first.

He turned off his flashlight, put it on the floor beside him, and put his head under the blankets.

He thought about that last line: the rocky coast and the sea. It was then that he realized what he wanted to do on his leave: go and find somewhere by the ocean.

# CHAPTER FIVE

The adjutant came out as the clerk was stamping Robbie's paperwork.

'So you're off to the Big Smoke. Don't forget to take your gas mask with you, never know what Jerry will get up to now he's got his back to the wall.'

Robbie checked his wallet: the two white fivers in the back compartment that he kept for emergencies were still there, together with another twelve pounds in notes. He was loaded. When he reached Bedford station he walked up the cobblestones and into the dusty wood-floored booking-office. He pushed his travel warrant under the glass to the clerk on the other side of the small window.

A smoky fire burnt without giving off heat in a cast-iron grate, and the place smelt damp, with a whiff of coal gas from the defunct lighting brackets.

He made his way on to the platform. Two grimy locomotives, so dirty that you could hardly see the LMS painted on their tenders, ground their way past, hauling a long train of low-loaders upon which tank after tank were chained, each with a white star painted on its turret. At the end of the train came the guard's van, with the guard standing in the doorway, one arm hooked round a handle.

The platform was densely packed by the time the signal by the redbrick road bridge at the end of the platform clanked up. The crowd edged forward in anticipation. In the distance a wisp of white steam and a dark shape appeared around a curve in the tracks, looming larger, developing into a red buffer bar and a round black boiler with a squat chimney.

The ground shook as the locomotive clanked past. The driver, in a blue work jacket with a greasy peaked cap, was leaning out of the gap between the engine and tender. With a scream of metal on metal the brakes came on and the train ground to a halt.

Carriage doors were opened and the struggle to get on began.

Robbie found himself halfway down one of the corridors. There was no hope of a seat. One American airman even ended up lying out on the luggage rack that ran above the seats. Porters signalled towards the front of the train. A piercing whistle sounded.

Nothing happened for a minute, then the carriage jerked forward. They would all have gone flying had they not been jammed so tightly that they only pushed embarrassingly into each others' faces.

An hour and a half later the train began to slide in and out of large brick-sided cuttings and short tunnels. Smoke from the engine enveloped the windows, through which could be caught glimpses of the famous red double-decker buses and trams crossing over bridges.

They rocked and lurched over points, then slowly began to enter the gloom of a large soot-stained terminus. With a squeal of brakes the train ground to a halt. People started jumping off and running down the platform even before it came to a halt.

He was in London again. His first visit had been brief, less than half a day, as he had arrived from home and then been dispatched on his way to training.

He had been excited then, because of what was happening, and also because he was setting foot in the city at the heart of the Empire.

But now it was the London of Maddie.

The excitement was different. And far greater.

At the end of the platform hundreds of people hurried in all directions as dirty-looking locomotives hissed and blew piercing jets of steam from their safety valves on top of the boilers up into the great vaulted roof.

He'd been given the name of a hotel by one of the Lancaster pilots at the airfield, which he'd managed to telephone. They were holding a room for him but he had to be there by two o'clock.

Emerging from the station Robbie blinked in the weak sunshine, taking in the bustling scene.

The famous double-decker red buses were everywhere, and trolley buses with their overhead arms connected to power lines, like trams, hummed quietly by. Black taxicabs, some with gas containers on their roofs, jostled for position with horse-drawn carts, many with old pneumatic car tyres for wheels.

He waited with crowds of service men and women until the traffic lights changed before they all surged across the road, mingling with city gents in bowler hats carrying rolled umbrellas.

There was an excitement and bustle in the air. News-stands carried something about Eisenhower, now Supreme Commander of the Allied Expeditionary Force.

Everybody was talking about when the Second Front – the invasion of Europe, might happen.

Eventually Robbie left the crowded pavements and found himself up a side street, gazing at his hotel. The entrance was protected by a wall of sandbags, now looking rather weathered and neglected. The windows were criss-crossed with brown paper strips to stop the glass flying inwards if a bomb fell nearby.

On either side of the brick building were bombsites, waste grounds full of rubble and weeds. The outlines of now non-existent rooms on the walls of the adjoining buildings, upon which the fireplaces, pictures and wallpaper were obscenely exposed in the sunlight, were pitiful testament to the lives of those who had once lived there.

The blitz was long over; he and so many others were now giving back tenfold what the Jerries had done in the early part of the war, though there were still raids, and even now people queued to spend the night in bunks on the platforms of the deeper parts of underground railway – the Tube.

Two silvery-grey barrage balloons rolled and swung slowly at their moorings set on the waste ground, looking, with their stabilizing fins, like legless elephants.

He stepped into a small drab reception lobby, where paint was peeling off the walls.

On her bicycle Maddie raced through the streets of central London, the tails of her headscarf flapping in the wind. She was eager to get home and change before her two-hour stint at the hotel – and then she would see Robbie. All day she had thought of meeting him again, of what would they do – and what might happen. As she weaved between other cycles and a stationary van, she was annoyed to be confronted by two policemen, checking identity cards, causing a queue. It would make her late.

When she eventually got home she changed quickly, freshening herself up with a quick body wash using the sink in her flat – there was no bath – before donning fresh knickers and a brassière. She drew on a pair of nylon stockings, part of a gift for giving a concert at an American Air Force hospital in East Anglia. It was luxury.

She rolled her hands up each thigh in turn to tighten the stockings, before attaching them to her suspender belt. She needed to use a sixpenny piece on one as the inner tab had broken off.

Normally she used old tea to brown her legs, and friends helped each other to draw a thin line at the back for the seam. Even ordinary thick stockings needed two coupons, out of her total of forty-eight.

From the middle drawer of a battered old chest that also served as a dressing-table she took out a plain white silk petticoat, her best one, sorting her arms through the straps before lifting it up and letting it fall down over her.

Maddie caught sight of her face, saw that it was flushed, and felt guilty.

It was the madness again. Far from abating, it had got worse. She still couldn't get over her behaviour – practically inviting him to come up to London.

She put on a white blouse and found a green tartan skirt that her friend's mother had made for her from an old curtain. With it buttoned up she smoothed the material over her hips, then started on her face, looking into the mirror that stood on the chest of drawers.

She had to steady her hand as she used the worn-down stub of her favourite lipstick, which she had been using very sparingly since 1941. It was getting dry and flaky, but she moistened her lips and applied a little more until she was satisfied.

It was a fifteen-minute walk to the hotel. Maddie pulled on her raincoat and grabbed her handbag and gas mask, then closed the front door behind her.

She reached Oxford Street where crossing by the John Lewis bomb site, she met a group of women pushing handcarts and dressed in boiler suits and headscarves. They were street cleaners returning from their shift, laughing raucously at some joke; the tips of their cigarettes glowed red in the dusk.

The piano was in the corner of the large bar, which was steadily filling up. She sat down and went straight into her first selection, starting with 'A Nightingale Sang in Berkeley Square'. As soon as she got halfway through 'Blue Moon' the first drink arrived.

Maddie nodded her appreciation towards the bar where a group of American naval officers whom she'd met before, grinned and waved back.

Later, when Maddie took her break, she looked around to see if there was any sign of him, but the room was now very crowded.

She mingled at the bar with the naval officers, accepting a light for the cigarette that she'd fished out of her bag.

'You're looking good – all dolled up. Are you playing for the Rossiters tonight?'

She often entertained for her supper at society parties, for which the cigarettes, drink and food came from 'Daddy's estate' and the always generous Americans. These parties made for a gay splash in a grey world of shortages. It was a good idea to be well known in circles that included patrons of the arts. When the war was over, as it must be some day, it might help to advance her career.

The Hon Freddie Rossiter, a captain in the Life Guards was just such a potential patron.

Maddie shook her head.

'Not tonight, Joe. I've got other plans.'

Maddie continued chatting with the Americans until it was nearly time to return to the piano. She made her way to the ladies to repair her make-up.

At the mirrors was a row of chattering giggling women, also restoring their faces.

'Did you get your nylons? My Yank gave me two pairs, darling.'

Maddie guessed what she might have had to do to earn them and it made her feel guilty about the ones on her own legs, though she had never done anything like that.

The girls prattled on, one saying:

'I'm going with Rick to see an ENSA show with some people from the Crazy Gang and have a meal afterwards at the Rainbow Corner. Gawd only knows what he'll make of Flanagan and Allen. I do hope they are in it.'

There were shrieks of laughter at the thought of the very British jokes and slapstick routines of the Crazy Gang, and the shaggy coat and battered straw hat of Flanagan as he sang 'Underneath the Arches' with Allen.

Back at the keyboard she flexed her fingers and started with 'As Time Goes By'.

The noise in the room had swollen to a roar, and only those in the immediate area could surely hear her. Playing with one hand she checked the time. Another half an hour to go before he was due.

That was when she looked up – and saw him.

# CHAPTER SIX

At last white smocks with winter hoods had arrived – just as the weather was changing. SS Haupsturmführer Walter Raus, as he now was, had left his neck strap undone as he scoured the horizon with his binoculars, watching in the distance the Russian infantry. In front of his unit thousands of Soviet troops and countless artillery pieces had been gathering strength for days.

He'd arranged his Panzer IIIs in a defensive position around a farm, the road to which ran through his lines.

When the first shells began dropping around him, he dived into a slit trench, right on top of somebody already in there – the medical officer.

Now the whole earth shuddered and rose up in great eruptions as rounds rained down on them, accompanied by the awful spine-chilling shrieks of the Katyusha batteries, nicknamed Stalin's Organs. They threw up batches of rockets in great streaks of flame.

How long it lasted he had no idea, being in a state of numb shock when he suddenly realized it had stopped. Cautiously he raised his head. What he saw made his blood freeze. Hundreds of Russian infantry were coming at them across the frozen ground, screaming 'URRAH URRAH'. Some were on rough little horses. He yelled out and his men started coming out of the very earth all around him.

The deafening crash of the high-explosive rounds of their panzers and flak wagons firing at point-blank range drowned out the unearthly whooping, then the hammering of machineguns and the hollow bang of grenades became non-stop.

And still the Russkies came on, were soon leaping into and over the shallow trenches. Hand-to-hand fighting raged, as enemy mortar shells fell amongst them, indiscriminately ripping apart German and

Russian flesh.

Terrified, mortally wounded horses, their bellies blown open, their white eyes bulging, screamed and kicked as they tried to get on their feet. Walter fired his machine pistol until there was no more ammunition, then used it as a club as yet another of the brown-uniformed figures leapt at him. They fell to the ground, clawing at each other's eyes, until Walter managed to smash the man's skull with a rock. The body was still twitching as he rolled off. Men were no longer human, but crazed demented creatures slithering in the reddening mud as they slashed and gouged and beat each other in the murderous struggle.

He staggered up and looked around at the weird figures bathed in the light of burning vehicles and wreathed in black oily smoke. If there was a hell, then it was here, on earth. As he bent to pick up a discarded rifle another Russian lunged at him, bayonet first. Before Walter could do anything, the man stiffened, dropped his rifle, a surprised look on his face, and collapsed into his arms – lifeless.

Walter let him drop to the ground. Beyond, a young grenadier, his gun still smoking, his white face streaked in blood and oil, looked blankly back at him, then was hidden from sight by a thick billow of smoke. After it rolled past he was lying on the ground, his uniform shredded on his bleeding body. It was thrown up like a rag doll by a second grenade.

Just when it seemed all was lost the battalion's heavy weapons, which had been rushed forward, opened up from the other side of the farm. The 21mm mortars and *nebelwerfers* brought death and destruction on the hordes still pouring up towards their barely held lines.

The 'howling' now came from their rockets whizzing overhead, and the air was filled with the rumbling of the heavy mortars, like summer thunder. The Russians were suddenly running away, back over the hundreds of bodies littering the ground.

In another two minutes the bombardment ceased. Exhausted grenadiers fired after them until Walter called out:

'Cease fire, cease fire.'

The cry was taken up by others until the only sound was the crackling of flames, the pitiful cries of the wounded, and the screaming horses.

Mercifully shots rang out and the horses were stilled.

After he'd checked his men and helped the medical officer and stretcher-bearers, he slumped down by a ruined wall.

Numb with exhaustion, fumbling, he found his water bottle, took a sip of the brackish, foul-tasting contents.

To him, it was as good as vintage champagne.

He took another sip, started to screw the cap back, but his fingers lost their grip.

It was more a loss of consciousness than sleep.

A shadow fell across Walter's face. With a reaction tuned by months of fighting, he was firing before he was conscious of what he was doing, hearing the man scream as he went down.

There had been no artillery this time, no frightening 'Urrahs.'

Another Russian in his dirty brown rags of a uniform came at him, firing a tommy gun, but dropped out of sight as Walter pumped a round into his belly.

Walter felt no pain, just a rush of blood down over his cheek. He realized he'd been hit by a bullet that had creased his forehead.

He brushed an arm across his face to clear his eyesight as an enemy T-34 tank crashed over the forward trenches, crushing screaming wounded of both sides beneath its tracks. Blood squelched into the mud.

One of his Panzer IIIs took it out with a round at point-blank range straight into the driver's hatch.

As the tank commander, body on fire, struggled out of the turret he was cut down by a burst from a machinegun.

A direct hit on the panzer that had just done the damage, caused it to explode in a ball of flame, ammunition shooting in all directions. More choking black smoke turned day into night as they fought on, using bayonets and spades to thrust and smash at the bodies jumping into the trenches.

It seemed to last for ever, then suddenly the Russians broke for a second time, were running back, the German machine guns reaping a bloody harvest. The remaining flak wagons swept the enemy mortar positions until they too, went quiet.

His chest heaving, he looked about him once more at the horrific scene. There was no doubt they would not survive a third attack – if it came. Countless dead, Russian and German, were strewn around in piles, while hundreds more were dotted on the approaches. Blood ran everywhere, enriching the soil.

He found SS Untersturmführer Werner's body surrounded by dead Russkies. His left arm had been blown off, the stump marked by a ragged field dressing, but his Luger pistol was still grasped in the other hand. He'd carried on fighting until he'd been overwhelmed and repeatedly bayoneted. Walter remembered seeing his proud parents the last time the regiment had paraded in Berlin.

Another young officer was lying on a stretcher, half of his face and cheek taken away by a grenade fragment, exposing his back teeth, which gave the macabre impression that he was grinning wildly.

Walter asked the orderly who was attending to him where the MO was. Without stopping his work the man nodded. 'Over there, sir.'

Walter's eyes fell upon the figure of his good friend, slumped down beside the body of the man he had been trying to treat. Both were dead.

It saddened him greatly. The doctor's wife, Marlene, was expecting their second child.

And so it went on.

Sergeants, platoon leaders: he counted so many that as a regiment they had almost ceased to exist. Now even the youngest soldiers had become veterans.

The loss of experienced officers in particular was taking on dangerous proportion. Now, nearly all the original company commanders with whom he had set out on the great crusade had been killed or wounded.

They were relieved later that day, and struggled back, the wounded riding on the few remaining tanks and wagons, until they reached an orchard where a support area had been established by the combat engineers.

He found a bunk in an underground bunker; the walls were made of tree trunks, the roof beams were covered with earth; his father, who had fought in the Great War, would have felt completely at home there. He began to write letters to the next-of-kin by the light of a single candle on an upturned crate.

Later in the week the news came through that they were being withdrawn from the Ost Front for rest and re-equipping; then they were going to be sent to strengthen Army Group B in France, where the long-awaited assault by the Anglo-Americans was expected. He would also get three weeks' leave. He couldn't wait to see Inge again.

But the Eastern front had one last horror for them before they reached a railhead. It was the aftermath of an attack by partisans.

They passed the scene in bitter silence. Live German prisoners had been bound over logs, their bowels dug out with bayonets, other comrades' faces held in the gaping wet entrails until they had suffocated, or drowned. Several had been tied upside down by their ankles to the tree branches, dowsed in gasoline, and burnt alive. Upside down the smoke did not choke them and so cut off their agony.

All the bodies had been castrated, including a row of badly wounded men who had been strangled as they lay on their stretchers.

As the terrible scene slowly fell behind, and went out of view, Walter Raus felt a dreadful anger. It was a ferocious, brutal war with immense loss of life. And because of the Allies' stupid insistence on unconditional surrender, Churchill and Roosevelt were in fact helping the Communist hordes into the heart of Europe. It didn't bear thinking about.

The journey back took over a week in an overloaded train that was frequently shunted into sidings so that many others, their coaches painted with red crosses on white circles could get past.

They were bringing home the thousands of wounded from the latest fighting. He saw some men on another train returning from leave eyeing them enviously, even the loss of a limb well worth being out of the hell that was the Ost Front.

But they did not envy those blinded, or gut shot, or the living torsos with no arms or legs, that were transported in rope baskets suspended from the roofs of the coaches.

Inge met him in Berlin. Although he'd cleaned up and been issued with a new uniform, the look on her face told its own story.

'Oh, my darling.'

Unusually for her she wrapped her arms around him in public, and just held on tight. He felt so much thinner than when he'd gone away, and his face was gaunt.

At last she stood back.

'I've got leave for your first week; after that I'm afraid I've got to go back to the hospital, we are so frightfully understaffed.'

He nodded. 'I expected as much. We'll try and find an apartment. Uncle Willie might be able to help.'

They walked arm in arm into the Berlin street, and boarded one of the city's yellow double-deck buses, which rattled and bumped down potholed streets. He gazed out of the window, shocked by the devastation. In some areas there were no buildings left standing; others were just skeletons pointing at the sky.

'My God, Inge, what is happening to us?'

She squeezed his arm.

'The bombing never stops, day or night.'

He turned and looked at her, searching her face as he said: 'Tell me – the truth now – how safe have you been?'

Inge shrugged. 'Don't worry. We have our own deep shelters, and there is a flak tower nearby. I sometimes go in there if I get caught out in the street.'

At least he knew that the huge communal shelters with their reinforced concrete, metres thick, were extremely safe.

'How long do you think the civilian population can take this?'

She looked away, out of the window.

'They're German – they'll manage.'

They passed a still-smoking ruin. Groups of rescue teams were toiling to bring out bodies. He noticed men under guard, in British Air force uniforms, sifting through the rubble and abused by passers-by.

He knew it was against the Geneva Conventions, but then, many of his brother officers had been worried by the Wehrmacht's abandonment of international law on the Ost Front – there were rumours of atrocities committed by the Sanderkommando in the rear areas.

It was war – total war. They'd barely got off the bus and started walking to her nurse's block when the sirens began their blood-curdling wail.

She took him by the hand and led him to a doorway guarded by a block gauleiter, who was ushering people into the shelter. He saluted Walter and pointed skywards.

'American gangsters, Hauptsturmführer.'

Inge woke from a deep sleep, her eyes slowly opening, seeing her sleeping husband beside her.

After a week in Erlangen, during which she had been feeding him up with fresh vegetables and meat from farming friends, he was looking better, especially in the face.

The days had passed sleeping in late, making love, walking in the woods, seeing their families and relatives.

There had even been a chance to go to the opera in Bamberg to see a touring company who were playing as part of Herr Goebbels' efforts to keep up public morale.

As they sat in their box, she had cast a surreptitious glance at her husband in his uniform, looking through opera glasses at 'Sophie' in *Der Rosenkavalier*.

He was so handsome, then as now, with the clear morning light from the open bedroom window falling on to his still sleeping face.

They had arrived back in Berlin, and were in an apartment on the Rankestrasse that belonged to the family of one of the nurses who had fled the bombing. Uncle Willie had found it. It was poorly lit, had dark heavy furniture, but was wonderful for them. They had explored all the rooms, from the kitchen with its large china cabinet, to the reception rooms with the pictures of the Führer, and the three bedrooms. Everywhere, great cracks ran in the plaster ceilings and walls, and the Führer had hung at an angle till Walter had straightened him. A large mirror over the fireplace had only half its glass still in the frame; all evidence of the heavy bombing.

The back windows were all boarded up, and through a chink they had seen a huge crater and the bare skeletons of the buildings opposite.

She sniffed. 'One of the English big bombs.'

That first night they had played hide and seek in the rooms, until he'd caught her and, laughing, screaming and kicking he had carried her to the bedroom.

Later, when the RAF came, and the night erupted into fury, they got up and went to the window. They stood there, Walter holding her with her back to him, looking out over the city – the capital city of the Third Reich, at the searchlights, and the streams of flak that trailed lazily upwards. Then came the enemy flares, nicknamed Christmas trees by the Berliners, great burning fingers of red, yellow and green slowly falling to earth.

Seas of fire began sweeping through whole districts.

And above it all sounded the steady unnerving drone of the enemy bombers. Suddenly Walter and Inge became aware of the noise of a diving plane, drawing nearer, engines screaming in overload.

Was it going to crash on top of them?

His arm around her tightened even more as he pulled her down to the floor and covered her with his body. He looked back up, out of the window.

The black silhouette of a twin-engined aircraft suddenly appeared against the flames of the burning city, passed right over them, and was gone. A Mosquito.

He kissed the top of her head, gently stroked her hair.

Would they survive?

Live life like a normal family?

In the morning, lying side by side, she became aware that his eyes were open, that he was staring at her, a little grin playing around that mouth she so loved.

He reached for her.

This was the best time, the dawn. The RAF had gone; it would be an hour or so before the Americans came.

Time to forget the terror of the night, time to renew their love.

# CHAPTER SEVEN

The train got into Penzance just as the dawn was showing in the eastern sky.

To John Fairfax it had seemed to take for ever, sitting in the dirty coach lit only by a blue light because of the blackout.

Around Exeter there had been an air-raid warning and they had come to a complete stop for nearly three quarters of an hour.

By this time he had seriously begun to wonder about his choice of destination; perhaps he should have gone to London like everybody else. But he had booked a room at a seaside pub which the American Red Cross had found for him; it had been a bit of a task, but somebody had recommended the Mermaid at a place called Port Gunn.

He walked with a group of bleary-eyed passengers, both navy and civilians and came out on to the forecourt.

When he enquired it turned out that Port Gunn was some fifteen miles back, eastwards, on the rocky southern coast.

He was turning away, making for the road that led up into the town, feeling not unhappy to walk there, when a man who'd just finished noisily off-loading galvanized metal milk churns and rolling them on their rims on to the platform called out: 'Excuse me, heard you asking – I'm going along the main road that way, take you to within a mile if you'd like a lift?'

John Fairfax didn't hesitate.

'Say, that's really kind of you.'

He threw his kitbag into the back and climbed into the old twenties-style cab. As they drove out of the town he could see the grey hulks of several corvettes caught in the early-morning light.

The man talked incessantly with a broad Cornish accent, complaining bitterly about the petty regulations of the Ministry of

Food, and the land girls he had quartered on him. Oh, they worked all right: it was the trouble that three young women brought with them – the boyfriends, the bickering, the women's problems and so on.

John listened with only half an ear, more interested in the country that was being unveiled as they bumped and lurched around tiny lanes, sometimes buried deep between banked hedgerows, at other times climbing up on to a gorse-and-heather covered moor that reminded him of scenes from the movie *Wuthering Heights* with the British actor Laurence Olivier. The illusion was further heightened by the louring clouds that seemed to be turning the newborn day back into night.

All of a sudden the heavens opened. The first spots of rain were the size of English pennies, in seconds merging into a solid downpour. The wipers clacked ineffectually back and forth. The window began to steam up. He helped clear it with his sleeve, only to see a torrent of water running down the glass as the rain drummed on the roof.

At least he couldn't hear the man's voice.

Outside, the road was now a turbulent stream. Across the hillside lightning forked to earth like the tongue of a celestial lizard.

The country was truly awe-inspiring. And then, just as suddenly as it had started, the rain stopped, the wipers grinding on a dry windshield.

The man switched them off.

'You're the lucky one, this is where you get out.'

They pulled up by a small lane that plunged down the hillside towards the sea.

John Fairfax shook his hand.

'Thanks again. I'd have been soaked.'

He jumped down, grabbed his bag from the back.

The man stuck his head out of his window.

'Enjoy your leave, son. All the best for the future.'

As he drove away the word 'future' seemed to linger for a moment in John's head, then he started down the steep lane, pausing after a moment or two to take in the view. The sea was now blue, the fern- and gorse-covered valley sharp and fresh after the storm. He took a deep breath of the sweet-smelling air and resumed his descent, sidestepping the bubbling streams that criss-crossed the asphalt as the rainwater drained off the hill.

The road turned sharply around a towering outcrop of rock, and there before him were the blue-slate roofs of Port Gunn, with its white cottages clinging to the ever steepening hillside until they grouped around the little harbour with a stone breakwater.

Several small inshore fishing boats, their hulls painted in bright colours, bobbed at their moorings. John's boots clumped on the cobblestone roadway, his footfalls ringing off the walls of the cottages.

Several women in dutch aprons and headscarves were sweeping steps and talking over low walls. They all stopped as he approached.

He grinned and called: 'Good morning, ladies. Am I right for the Mermaid?'

One of them pointed down the street.

'At the bottom, you can't miss it. Are you staying there?'

'Yep.' He touched his finger to his cap. 'Thank you, ma'am.'

He carried on, leaving the women looking after him. One nudged the other.

'Him looks like that Tyrone Power. See you in the Mermaid tonight, then?'

With a push of her broom the other woman grinned.

'Half the women of the village will be down there what with all the men-folk away in the navy.'

The Mermaid was on the waterfront, grey-stoned, its blue-painted woodwork weathered and peeling. The door stood open, revealing a gloomy interior.

Above the door a sign of a mermaid on a rock, creaked gently in the breeze.

He stepped in on to the stone floor. The place smelt of stale beer and cigarette smoke. There was nobody in sight. He could hear beer barrels being rolled and upended.

'Hello there, anyone around?' he called out. A man came from the back, wiping his hands with a cloth.

'Ah, you're the American visitor – that right?'

Standing there in his uniform John Fairfax grinned and nodded. 'Guess so.'

The man prattled on.

'We get a lot of people down from London for a couple of days – newly-weds, that sort of thing, and those who just want to get away from the bombing. Can't say we've had a Yank before – begging your pardon.'

When John Fairfax was eventually shown to his room, up a twisting, creaking staircase, he found it spartan but clean. The bed was covered in a green candlewick spread and there was an old brown wardrobe and a chest of drawers. He went to the window, where the floral curtains were lifting with the breeze coming off the sea.

The view was of the harbour, where seagulls swooped and screamed over the boats.

Tired as he was, he decided to freshen up and go for a walk. When he came back down into the bar, he'd changed into a woollen roll-neck sweater and cord trousers, bought from a lady in Cirencester who'd advertised them in the paper. Her husband had been killed at Tobruk. The publican was washing glasses. He looked up and grunted.

'You look different.'

John felt different. It was the first time he'd been out of uniform for months.

He asked, 'Which way for a good walk?'

Five minutes later he'd reached the end of the harbour wall and was climbing up a dirt path towards the top of the cliff, looking down at the rock pools and seaweed left by the receding tide.

As soon as he reached the top of the path the wind caught him, buffeting him as he turned along the crest of the hill until he was confronted by a wide bay of yellow sand with white surf rolling in on to the shore from a blue-green ocean. John Fairfax felt his heart lighten.

This coast was more rugged than Maine's, the cliffs were bigger, and treeless moors swept the skyline. But the sea – was the sea.

As he started down another path, he suddenly became aware of a tiny figure moving along the shoreline, stopping occasionally to stoop and pick something up.

As he got lower, and the figure came nearer, he realized it was a woman; her dress was rippling against her slim body, and around her neck she wore binoculars. Like a young girl, she was holding her sandals in her hand, splashing her feet in the shallows. He reached the beach and jumped the last few feet on to the sand, avoiding a coil of rusting barbed wire. He set off along the flat, aware that she had suddenly seen him.

Even as they drew nearer the sound of the surf and the wind prevented any greeting from a distance. They were right on top of each other before he could see her face clearly, her green eyes bored into him with startled interest. Then he was aware of more, of the blonde hair dancing wildly around a beautiful face, a face that was doing something to his senses.

She saw a tall dark-haired stranger – she had never seen him around there before – good-looking in a rugged youthful way and with an athletic bearing.

Was he an enemy agent? There was no one around if he decided to do anything to her.

Then all fear vanished as he said, 'Hi there, bit of a rough day.'

His soft drawl took her completely by surprise. Her relief was obvious.

'You're an American.'

Smiling, he shrugged. 'Guilty as charged.'

'Oh.' She pulled a lock of hair from her eye. 'I'm sorry, that sounded funny. I didn't mean to be rude.'

He said something, but in reality he was so taken by her presence that he had no idea what it was.

John Fairfax suddenly forgot the war, forgot home – forgot everything.

It was as if he had not existed before that moment.

# CHAPTER EIGHT

Robbie Cochran looked down at the North Sea, shining like molten silver with patches of lead caused by the shadows of scattered clouds in the moonlit sky, until a darker line appeared in the forward view.

The R/T crackled. 'Enemy coast ahead,' reported Davey.

The probing beams of the enemy long-range early warning radar would now be detecting them.

In their fast, high-flying 'Mossie' F-for-Freddie, they felt, at this stage, relatively safe. Their moment would come over the target: Berlin.

They droned on in the darkness, able to see towering clouds in the moonlight, Robbie checking the Oboe directional signal in his earphone that was taking them to their target.

His mind wandered – to Maddie.

He still could not get over what had happened.

He was early, but he couldn't wait any longer. He'd wasted time in a news and cartoon cinema, but now as he mounted the steps of the hotel he paused. There was an awful lot of noise. The place was heaving with people. Then he caught the tinkle of a piano.

After seeing her in concert at Bedford, it seemed a bit of a comedown. Robbie edged his way into the crowd, struggling past uniformed men with pint glasses in one hand, the other arm around a girl's waist, having a party, he realized, with a frenzy – for who knew what tomorrow would bring? Suddenly the crowd parted and there she was, caught in the light from the lamp on the piano, looking stunning in her tartan skirt and white blouse. She saw him at the same time – and ceased playing. Nobody noticed in the scrum, until an American soldier leaned over.

'Hey, honey. I was enjoying that.' She blinked, and resumed, still looking at Robbie, who came right up to her.

'You're early.'

He leaned on the piano.

'I know, do you mind?'

She carried on playing, looking up at him from time to time.

Maddie felt her heart beat faster. Despite his strong face there was something boyish and vulnerable about him.

She suddenly chuckled, white teeth biting her lower lip, and began playing 'Just The Way You Look Tonight'.

When she'd finished it she said, 'Last one,' and started on 'When Irish Eyes Are Smiling'.

At last, with a final sweep of her hand up the keys, she stopped playing. There was a cheer from the regulars who knew her repertoire.

She gave a little bow to left and right, then started to gather up her pieces of music.

'It's been a long day.'

She saw his face fall, but before she could say anything to reassure him that she was looking forward to the rest of the evening, a group of British and American officers, including a colonel and a couple of majors crowded around.

'Maddie, we're going to Jimmy Gee's – are you coming?'

He felt an instant stab of jealousy, but she shook her head.

'No, Piers, not tonight.'

There were groans of disappointment and attempts to get her to change her mind, with some suspicious glances at the young flight lieutenant who was obviously hanging around her.

'You OK Maddie? Need a lift or anything?'

It was one of the protective Americans – the colonel.

'No, no thanks, Grant. I'm fine, really. Will you be at the Wigmore Hall concert?'

'You betcha. See you there then. Goodnight.'

Robbie must have looked crestfallen because she took hold of his hand.

'Come on, I've got to collect my raincoat, then we can go.'

She didn't know where it came from, but she was tired as she added hesitantly: 'How about coming home, it's only a short walk? We could have fish and chips and listen to the radio . . .' she faltered, 'only if you'd like to of course.'

He tried not to sound too eager.

'Suits me.'

Anxiously she asked, 'Are you sure? We could still get into one of the shows if you wish – or the cinema?'

Quickly Robbie said, 'No, no – really. I'd like nothing better.'

Maddie nodded.

'Thank you. I really don't want to be in crowds of people tonight, but I do so want to spend the evening with you.'

He felt as if he must be in a dream from which he would wake up with a jolt at any moment.

A commissionaire held the last blackout door for them and they went outside, into the centre of one of the biggest cities in the world. It was pitch black, but already her arm was threading through his own as she said 'Mind the steps – there are four.'

It felt wonderful, having her holding on to him as they started along the street.

'Watch out for the lampposts, girls have been known to come into work in the morning with whopping shiners and said they'd walked into one in the blackout.' She chuckled. 'At least that's what they say happened.'

'You think they got it some other way?'

Her arm gave a gentle tug.

'Of course; boyfriends or husbands.'

'That's terrible.'

His innocence was genuine, he truly meant it.

She squeezed his arm affectionately.

Robbie asked: 'How do you find living in London?'

'Very different from home. It's big, shabby and exciting all at the same time.'

As if to underline the exciting part, searchlights suddenly flickered into life and started to sweep the night sky in the east, followed by a few far-off muffled thumps.

Realizing he might not know what was happening, despite being in the Air Force, she explained with all the experience of one who lived in London.

'Anti-aircraft batteries. Might be a lone raider – nuisance raids have become quite a feature these past nights, not like the blitz of a year or two ago. That's because of what you RAF lads are doing.'

He shrugged.

It was true in one way. Air Chief Marshal Bomber Harris had been as good as his word with formations of over a thousand on some raids. The German aircraft industry was now totally focused on fighter production in defence of the Reich.

Another explosion sounded. This one had more of a *crack* to it. He felt Maddie's hand tighten on him.

Obviously that one had not been just ack-ack.

They emerged into a square just as the moon rose clear of the clouds, flooding everything in a pale blue light.

Instantly there was a chorus of wolf whistles from a group of Yanks gathered around a bench drinking. He passed her to his other arm, and hurried on.

'Hello, air force. You want a turn?'

It came from a woman with peroxided hair, wearing a very short skirt and low-cut blouse, who took absolutely no notice of Maddie as she continued: 'Five bob for the works, luv, half-a-crown for anything else.'

His cheeks burned with embarrassment. Mortified, he just kept on walking.

Suddenly he heard a giggle. It was Maddie.

'Terrible, isn't it?'

He shook his head in disbelief. To hear about the Piccadilly commandoes was one thing, to actually experience them was quite another.

He winced. 'Is it like this all the time?'

'Afraid so. You get used to it.'

But worse sights were to come as they walked on.

When they eventually reached Oxford Street, Maddie reassured him. 'All this ends here.'

He was relieved. The shadows had been alive with the sounds of supposedly aroused women and grunting men.

And all of it with her by his side.

Thank God for the dark.

There was a small queue inside the chip shop. He watched as a new block of white lard was dumped into the boiling fat, spitting and bubbling as it danced around, shrinking.

When it was her turn she asked for two rock salmon and chips, and a halfpen'orth of scraps – the bits of batter sieved out of the fat. Fish was one of the few things that wasn't rationed, thanks to the bravery of the trawlermen.

The man sloshed on a load of salt and vinegar before wrapping the two portions from a pile of neatly cut newspaper sheets.

Robbie insisted on paying.

He came out of his memory with a jolt.

Davey had touched his arm, was pointing at tracer fire twinkling in the distance. They were beginning to overhaul the main bomber force, and it was being attacked by German night fighters.

Suddenly fire streamed back, enveloping the fuselage of a Lancaster. The plane began to fall away to earth, gathering speed on its downward plunge.

There was a brief flash, then the ground was lit by a dim glow. He doubted if anybody had got out; seven men dead who had been alive only a few minutes before; seven families yet to hear the devastating news.

Battle was joined. It was going to be a long night. His guts began to churn.

Another five minutes elapsed, and then ahead the sky was abruptly lit by one searchlight going straight up. It was a radar-guided master light.

'Here we go.'

No sooner had he said it than the master light tilted over, found a bomber. Immediately the night was pierced by scores more slave lights that coned the unfortunate Lancaster.

Flak started to fly up, red bursts so dense it seemed impossible for anything to survive in it. There was no noise, other than the roar of their own engines. Suddenly in the sky ahead a target indicator bomb exploded in a great cluster of sixty yellow flares, burning with an intensity like miniature suns, that turned into brilliant trails of fire drifting down so slowly that they seemed almost to be stationary. It was the first pathfinder's sky marker, followed almost immediately by ground target indicators burning bright green.

The first wave of bombers flew straight into the heavy concentration of flak and by now a host of searchlights. The master bomber, circling above, directed them to bomb the green markers. Robbie heard his dispassionate voice on the radio repeating, 'I say again, bomb the green markers, bomb the green markers.' The searchlights began to cone several Lancasters, catching them starkly against the dark sky. As the radar-controlled flak zoomed in on them they began to dive and weave, desperate to get out of the light. Hundreds of angry red points bursting immediately into black puffs of smoke, spread all around them.

A plane started to go into a spin, one wing torn off by an explosion; it drifted away as the main part of the Lancaster went into a steep dive and disappeared from view. By now the first bombs were raining down, hundreds of twenty- and forty-pound incendiaries throwing out lumps of benzyl and rubber that burned so fiercely they sucked oxygen out of the surrounding air. These were mixed with huge block-busting explosives, their hits showing as beads of intense white light that expanded in an instant in a widening circle to the horizon.

Soon, conflagrations were raging over an area of several square miles. Another Lancaster exploded, its fuel tanks racing to earth like blazing meteors.

Davey had been listening to the Oboe transmission, and now the pattern of dots and dashes merged, confirming they were at their bombing point. Hunching forward into the nose, Davey pressed the tit on the release and disgorged the load of red flares – target indicators – which fell clear.

The squadron's job was to neutralize the creep-back effect of less experienced bombers who had prematurely dropped their loads in the face of the fierce, heavy flak.

Robbie pushed the yoke forward and boosted the engines, diving and banking away. Through the roar of the engines they heard a sound like gravel being thrown at the fuselage. Both knew it was flak hitting them.

They raced low across a city that was a cauldron of fire, so bright that they were clearly in view as they crossed the streets at less than 1,000 feet, buffeted by the updraught from the fires that raged into the sky like the surface of the sun. They could see in incredible detail the streets and houses beneath them. Above and behind them their flare bombs burst into brilliant red candles drifting down above the stricken city.

Suddenly the aircraft jumped as if it had hit something hard. Shaken, he pulled back on the yoke, breathed a sigh of relief as she responded, climbing away from the man-made inferno below.

The master bomber's still unruffled voice came over the R/T as the final wave of 240 aircraft came in.

'Bomb the red markers, bomb the red markers. I say again, bomb the red markers.'

Davey set the course for Little Staughton. They left the battle raging behind them, overtaking bombers straining for home, some limping on two or three engines, to be harassed all the way by the night fighters.

After half an hour, with things remaining quiet, he felt his heart rate slow. His mouth was dry, his lips cracked.

They said nothing, except when Davey ordered a course change to avoid a known flak area.

They roared on through the dark, every minute bringing them nearer to safety – something that well over 150 airmen wouldn't make that night.

Though he didn't know it, it was the last time he would take part in the strategic bombing of Germany.

# CHAPTER NINE

The moment came when they had to part. At least this time Inge felt relief that he was going to France. Whatever the dangers that had to be faced, it must be better than going back East.

She straightened the Knight's Cross around his neck.

'Nevertheless you will take care, won't you, darling?'

He smiled. 'I'm a soldier Inge, a grenadier. I have to do my job, but,' to satisfy her as he saw her frown he continued, 'we are only re-equipping and training. If and *when* the Anglo–Americans attempt to land we will push them back into the sea very quickly, you wait and see. Everybody's ready.'

He meant it. Rommel had updated the defences of the Atlantic Wall, as well as the strategy and tactics that were to be deployed in its defence.

They were ruthlessly to throw the Allies back before they had time to establish a coherent bridgehead.

The expected landing would be in the Pas de Calais area – the coast nearest to England, but, in order to try and cover every eventuality, the panzers had to be able to reach several possible sites, so they were being held inland, in reserve. But they would have to move quickly.

She smiled in relief, changed the subject.

'Now, are you sure you have everything – plenty of clean handkerchiefs and socks. . . ?'

He squeezed her hand.

'Yes, yes.'

Inge came up on to her toes and gave him a very chaste kiss on the lips.

She had never known such happiness as they had enjoyed during the last couple of weeks. Despite the bombings they had, for the first time, enjoyed a proper home life of their own, with nobody else in the house. She had shopped for food and cooked their meals, albeit sometimes on a foul-smelling oil stove when the electricity was off, which was often. She had delighted in their evenings, finding him his pipe and slippers and snuggling up together on one of the old sofas as he read to her stories, mostly German classics, but her favourite was a translation of Margaret Mitchell's *Gone With The Wind*.

Sometimes they went to the cinema, – in the late afternoon, after the Americans had gone and before the Tommies arrived.

Having experienced the bombings at first hand Walter had renewed, desperately, his pleas for her to give up the nursing in Berlin and go to the country. He'd felt guilty, since he himself believed so strongly in duty: to the regiment, to the division, to the Fatherland. But he convinced himself that asking Inge to leave Berlin was just what a caring husband would do; he had a duty to protect his loved ones, his family. And the Fatherland depended upon its families.

However, Inge, who had been brought up in the League of German Maidens believed equally in service and duty, and that meant remaining with her patients.

In bed one night he had pointed out that she had been taught that her role was to be a mother of Germany's future warriors. She had pointed out, with a growing physical confidence in her role of wife and lover and slipping a hand beneath his cool man parts, that she was not as yet expecting a young warrior and what was he going to do about it?

That had ended the discussion for that night.

But next morning, as she slid out of his still sleeping embrace and went to the lavatory, she couldn't help but think of what had been drummed into her in the League, that her overriding duty was to be the nucleus of a family. It worried her that as yet nothing had happened.

The Führer himself had told them at one of their rallies that 'Whilst the man sacrifices fighting for his people, the woman sacrifices in fighting to maintain his people.'

At school she had also been taught racial awareness, and never a year passed without incessant reminders of their racial duties to the 'National Community'.

But in the last year, despite the party's efforts to suppress any dissent, for the first time people had dared to joke about their leaders.

At first Inge had been utterly shocked when she'd heard young nurses who'd been at the racial awareness lectures joking that the perfect German was as blond as Hitler, as slim as Goering and as tall as Goebbels.

She'd put that down to the strain they were all under, the dry humour of the Berliners in response to the incessant bombing.

It really started coming home to her, though, that attitudes were changing when her own husband, over a bottle of wine in Erlangen, had told her the jokes his brother officers – even in the SS – were making as they performed miracles of self-sacrifice and feats of arms on the Eastern Front.

Walter had chuckled as he told her the story of two friends talking. 'When this war is over,' says one, 'I plan to take a bicycle tour around Germany.'

His friend replies, 'Fine, and what will you do after lunch?'

Walter had shaken his head.

'Good – yes?'

Inge had grinned weakly; she really hadn't heard him talk like this before, and she looked nervously around.

But what really chilled her, she who, like all the girls of her generation, had been in thrall to the Führer, was hearing the joke the troops were telling each other since the news of the fall of Stalingrad and the complete annihilation of the Sixth Army – they who had led the victory parade through the Arc de Triomphe. 'Here's another,' said Walter, pouring himself another generous measure of wine before apologizing and topping up her glass, 'What's the difference between the sun and Hitler?'

'The answer?' Walter had smiled grimly over his glass and told her. 'The sun rises in the east while the Führer goes down in the east.'

Her blood ran cold with the realization that her husband, and obviously many in the armed forces were already contemplating the fact that someone she thought of as invincible, who could do no wrong, who had shaped her whole life until then, was after all not the god he had appeared to be.

It just didn't seem possible.

She recalled when Hitler had spoken at the rallies. It had been heart-stopping. She had remembered how the girls in the League had been held back by smiling party officials and policemen as they all strove to be near to the man who had led their nation out of the wilderness and humiliation of the post-war years to become a great power again.

Inge and all her friends, and her mother and all her friends, had adored him for what he had done.

He had restored order and put food on the table. No woman could ask for more.

Some had said it was a catastrophe when the war broke out, but even they were soon silenced by the Führer's miraculous victory: he was seen on a newsreel in the cinema looking at the Eiffel Tower from a Paris vantage point, and all after the lightning offensive that was the modern blitzkrieg.

It had to be said that she had really enjoyed being in the League of German Maidens.

They had camped, sung songs, tracked for miles through forests and over hills, and done all sorts of exciting, practical things.

So Inge felt bewildered, and disappointed with the way things were going. It was as if her childhood, with all its comforting security, was being eroded away. She clung on to her past in desperation, and until the day she was ordered otherwise she would stay at her post; duty required it, as she reminded him.

Faced with her determination, Walter had reluctantly and guiltily given in. Duty was what they were all about as good Germans.

A whistle sounded.

He touched her chin, ran the back of his hand gently over her cheek.

'I have to board now, darling. Please write to me – tonight. Your letters are a great inspiration and comfort to me.'

With that he cupped his hands around her face, kissed her lips, then her forehead, before tearing himself away.

More whistles sounded. Slowly the carriage began to move. He reappeared at a window, staring back at her, motionless, framed by the glass and wood as if he were a photograph, a photograph moving steadily away from her as the train picked up speed. Eventually he was lost in a cloud of steam and smoke.

By the time it had dispersed she could no longer see into the individual windows.

Feeling terribly lonely she turned and made for the exit, just as the sirens started up their dreadful moaning wail.

It suited how she felt in her soul.

# CHAPTER TEN

The journey home was relatively safe for them in the high flying, fast, Mosquito.

Nevertheless, you could never be sure, not until you saw the coast of East Anglia.

Robbie fumbled under the side of his seat and extracted the sandwiches and his thermos that the WAAFS had prepared.

As he unhitched his oxygen mask and took a sip to refresh his dry mouth after hours of breathing in oxygen, he couldn't help think again of that week in London.

She stopped abruptly and pushed the fish-and-chip packets into his hands.

'Here, hold these.'

He stood in the dark until a weak light from her torch lit up a lock and he saw her hand insert a key.

Maddie made sure he was in the little hall before closing the door and drawing the blackout curtain. She switched on the light.

Robbie found himself in a small linoleum-floored area with flaking whitewashed walls and with ascending steps covered in carpet, with brass stair-rods running across the full width.

She led the way, Robbie feeling guilty as he took in her slim nylon-covered legs right in front of his eyes, with the thin seam running up the back.

The old boards creaked under their weight.

At the top there was a landing that led into a small room with a white-painted wooden fireplace surrounding green tiles in which was set a gas fire.

An old sofa and a battered easy chair were arranged around it with a brown, ring-stained coffee table in the middle.

To the left the curtain that could be pulled to close off the kitchen was open, revealing a deep white sink, a wooden draining-board and an ancient gas cooker in chipped blue and white enamel paint. Maddie pushed past the sofa to the small sash window and hurriedly pulled the curtains.

'We've got a vicious ARP warden – even now. Put the fish and chips on the draining-board, and take a seat.'

He did as he was told, then walked behind the sofa, between it and a brown sideboard, stopping to look at the photographs on top.

From the direction of the kitchen, he could hear water from the tap as it roared into the blackened kettle, which she placed on the top of the cooker. With Swan Vesta matches she lit the gas with a faint plop.

'It will take a little while. The pressure is very low these days.'

She turned and saw him looking at her photographs.

'That's my mother and father.'

It was a picture of a World War One soldier in British Army khaki and puttees, and a woman whom he had instantly identified as her mother, dressed in Edwardian-style clothes, sitting before her husband on a chaise longue. An aspidistra on a jardinière stood to one side.

Frowning, she came over and took it gently from him, studied it for a moment then set it back down.

'We were part of the British Empire in those days.'

She didn't offer anything further and returned to the kitchen. He watched her take down plates from a wooden rack and open a drawer to get out knives and forks.

He moved on, turning at the end of the sofa, noticing a door just beyond the sideboard. It was ajar, and he could see a brown headboard with a patchwork bedspread and white pillows.

They ate in front of a gas fire that seemed at first to take heat out of the little room, not warm it.

When they were finished she collected the empty plates.

'Are you absolutely sure you didn't mind doing this? You must have had more exciting things on your mind for leave?'

He shook his head.

'Not at all. I haven't spent an evening in a home really since leaving New Zealand.'

Concerned, she asked, 'Do you miss it a lot?'

He thought for a second, then nodded.

'Yes, I suppose I do – especially when we get leave.'

'Tell me about it.'

Surprised, he looked at her, realized she really meant it.

'I grew up on a farm outside Christchurch and went to school in the city when I was eleven.'

He looked wistful as he added, 'Money was tight but my elder brother and I had the run of the farm and the surrounding hills, sometimes camping out for days on end. We would ride, shoot and fish, and swim in the rivers. Couldn't have asked for a better life.'

He shook his head, 'Ran wild really, except when the old man took his strap to us.'

He chuckled at the memory. Obviously it had been said with nostalgic affection for his father.

Maddie frowned. Her own memories were not so loving, but he didn't notice the sudden hardness in her face.

He continued: 'My brother was all set to take over the farm, I was going to be a surveyor, when the war in Europe broke out. So we all joined up – naturally.'

Maddie was puzzled.

'But why?'

He grinned, shrugged.

'Because the mother country was in trouble, that's why.'

She shook her head in disbelief. Ireland had struggled so long to be free from the 'mother country'.

'Why did you go into the air force?'

'As a kid I used to fly a Tiger Moth.'

When he saw that she didn't understand, he added: 'It's a two-seat biplane.'

'Gosh, I thought you said money was tight. Are your family rich?'

He laughed.

'Good lord, no. A man kept it in one of our barns. He used to take me up for joy rides when I was eleven – let me try the controls. I went solo when I was fourteen. He thought I was sixteen.' He laughed. 'Dad was furious, until he realized I could go and check on the livestock up in the hills in half the time.'

There was a pause, which he broke with: 'And you? Tell me about your life?'

It was her turn to shrug.

'Not much to tell. Grew up in a small Irish town. Wasn't above average at anything really, except music and the piano. We were – are – very poor, but I got a scholarship.'

She suddenly grinned. 'Come and look at this.'

She put the plates down and went to the bedroom door, pushed it open, waited as he slowly came around the sofa. His eyes fell on the bed. His embarrassment was painfully obvious.

She chuckled, a low husky sound that stirred his blood.

'No – not that, silly – this. . . .'

She disappeared around the door. The next moment he heard the piano.

With one hand on the edge of the door he looked around. An old upright was jammed tightly into the space and Maddie was standing as she played it. From its front board two metal candelabra held half-used candles. Sheet music was piled everywhere, on the piano, on the floor under the bed.

She glanced up at him, eyes shining.

'Do you know this one?'

He nodded. He'd heard the gently rolling notes many a time when his sister practised it.

'*Für Elise*.'

He stood beside her as she played a few more bars, watching her slim forearms and long tapered fingers moving effortlessly over the yellow keys.

Robbie was also aware of her perfume. A small silver bracelet caught the light from the overhead bulb with its white shade.

After a few more seconds, she suddenly swept her knuckles across the keyboard, finished with a flourish and turned to face him.

He was so close their bodies touched. Nervously she ran her tongue over her lower lip – then the 'madness' erupted without warning.

She reached up and held on to his head, kissing all around his face as he pulled her roughly to him, at last seizing her mouth with his.

It lasted for what seemed ages as he drank in her sweet taste before she tore herself away, her hands frenziedly smoothing down her skirt, face flushed.

Robbie was shaken.

'I'm sorry. I'd better go.'

Feeling wretched he grabbed his cap and coat, and made for the stairs.

Maddie called: 'What time tomorrow?'

He paused, turned, his heart in his mouth.

'Tomorrow?'

She put one hand on the back of a chair to steady herself, her legs were shaking.

She nodded. 'Come at ten o'clock – please.'

He looked down at the cap in his hand, murmured, 'Thank you,' then started down the stairs. Maddie followed.

Neither of them felt they should kiss again. She opened the door and he went out into the darkness.

She called, 'Goodnight' after him and added: 'I've got to close the door – the blackout.'

He waved his hand to show he understood.

She closed it, and leaned back, her heart racing, still feeling weak.

What was it about him that had got to her so much?

Handsome young men were two a penny in London at the moment.

But there was something.

And she began to realize that she might no longer be in control of her own destiny.

# CHAPTER ELEVEN

Making the excuse that he felt tired after his journey John Fairfax did not continue but returned to the village with the young woman. Both were aware that something was happening between them.

Sally Dytham walked beside the tall American, conscious of his interest, whilst he strove to keep his eyes off her, to avoid appearing rude, but it was difficult.

By the time they reached the first houses, and had started to walk along the front by the fishing boats, he was bold enough to ask: 'Do you live here?'

She pointed at a small cottage at the far end of the village, set apart from the other whitewashed buildings.

'That's my place. I'm renting it for a couple of weeks.'

Surprised, he exclaimed, 'Oh, so you're not local?'

She shook her head. 'Dear me no. As far as the locals are concerned, although they're polite, I get the impression they suspect that I might be a German spy. There are always U-boat sightings by the fishermen, especially after a Saturday night in the pub.'

'And are you?'

She laughed. 'I thought you were one coming along the beach.'

He frowned, looked theatrically stern and shook his head.

'It's very suspicious, a woman on her own – *and* with binoculars.'

Sally knew he was being funny but she spoke without thinking.

'My fiancé was killed in the Battle of Britain. Why on earth would I be on their side?'

John Fairfax knew his face had gone brick-red. He stammered.

'Oh, I'm – I'm terribly sorry.'

They walked on in uncomfortable silence before she suddenly said: 'I'll be in the Mermaid tonight at about seven o'clock.'

She didn't add any more, but the implication was obvious.

His heart lifted. As they were outside the Mermaid at that moment, he stopped.

She kept going.

Nothing more was said. He watched her walking away.

Back in his room he stripped off, had a wash in the small communal bathroom, then lay on his bed thinking of her. She had stirred all sorts of emotions in him.

If she didn't come to the pub tonight he would seek her out somehow, even if it meant hanging around the shore near her cottage, like a bloody adolescent.

He grunted at his use of the British swear-word.

She let herself into the cottage. The front door opened straight into the main room with its open fireplace, chintzy sofa and two easy chairs, grandfather clock and a gramophone on a cabinet.

Sally Dytham went through to the small kitchen, poured herself a glass of water and gulped it down. She drew another one, carried it into the sitting room and sat down.

She felt awful, guilt threatened to overwhelm her.

She was actually trembling slightly. Since David she had not so much as looked at another man, hadn't wanted to know, until now. . . .

Then, with no warning, like a damned god, one walks as if out of the sea itself.

She'd heard of love at first sight, hadn't believe it.

Still didn't want to.

But it was no good.

As she took another sip of water she realized that from what he had told her he was on leave. He would be going back . . . to what? She had already lost one man to the war.

Sally Dytham sat there, her mind in a turmoil. But one thing started becoming clearer. When she met him again she would waste no time. They had no time.

Nobody had time any more.

There were several people in the bar, mostly older men but there were one or two women.

They all stopped talking when he walked in, having had his supper in a back room, of fresh fish simmered in milk and butter with hunks of white bread.

He nodded at them and received acknowledgment. The publican, leaning on his elbows talking to a customer, stood up.

'Was everything all right?'

John Fairfax pulled himself on to a stool.

'Perfect, lovely fish.'

The man nodded.

'Landed this morning. What'll it be?'

He nodded at the pump handle before him.

'A pint of that, please.'

As he watched the publican drawing on the handle, letting it return to the upright with a clunk, and repeating the process as the glass filled with the dark liquid, the conversation in the room resumed.

He glanced at his watch. Ten to seven. He wondered whether she came regularly into here – alone.

He'd heard that in general women in England didn't enter pubs without a man escorting them.

But come she did.

John Fairfax's jaw dropped as Sally, unannounced, slipped on to the stool beside him. She had put on a touch of lipstick and powder, was wearing a soft cashmere sweater and a skirt, and had tied a silk scarf around her neck. A black-and-white herringbone tweed coat was thrown casually over her shoulders.

To him she was the epitome of a very classy English woman.

He managed: 'You look wonderful.'

'Thank you.'

After a pause she put her head to one side and asked teasingly, 'May I have a drink?'

Embarrassed, John Fairfax said, 'I'm sorry – of course. What will it be?'

Sally looked at the hovering publican and nodded. 'The usual please, Sam.'

When it came it turned out to be a pink gin. She raised the glass.

'To your good health.'

He took his half-drunk pint and clinked it against hers.

'And yours.'

He got out his cigarettes, offered her one.

She took it and he lit her up, watching as she blew out smoke from her red lips.

'Do you come in here regularly? I mean, the way you spoke . . .'

She smiled and nodded.

'You could say that, couldn't you, Sam.'

The publican chuckled as he dried a glass.

'Ay.'

Puzzled, he waited for her to explain. She was obviously enjoying herself, and her mischievous twinkling eyes captivated him.

'It's the telephone. I keep in touch with my family, and my unit.'

That did set him back. 'Unit?'

'I'm in the WRNS – do you know of them?'

John Fairfax was well used to the women in their dark, navy-blue uniforms; often they were employed as drivers to high-ranking Royal Naval officers who came to the liason and planning meetings at the camp.

'Yes.'

She saw he was utterly bemused.

'I joined up after David was gone. I've got a month's leave at the moment. They thought I needed a rest but I have to keep in touch in case they need to call me in. It's hard on the girls, especially those on the wireless; they often hear dreadful things, you see.'

She added no more, but asked about him, so he told her about his home and family, and arriving in England.

Sally finished her drink.

She knew then that the moment had come, and that she felt more strongly than ever that what she was about to do was the right thing; that she was, if anything, even more strongly attracted to this man, this boy, for that was what they all were. She slid off the stool, gathered her coat around her shoulders, and looked up into his anxious eyes as he said:

'You're not going, are you?'

She nodded, put her arm through his, quite uncaring about the hush that had suddenly overcome the room.

'And so are you.'

# CHAPTER TWELVE

The château was set in its own grounds, a magnificent eighteenth century building with the typical turrets of its French region. It was set at the end of a long drive that meandered through the rolling hills of the estate.

It was now the headquarters of the new division and the big red, white and black swastika banner hung down inside the portico. Beside the door stood the divisional flag.

Amongst the trees of the surrounding woods tanks, new and old, were being refitted, tested, prepared for war.

SS Haupsturmführer Walter Raus, dressed in his vulcanized long raincoat, crunched across the gravel, answered the salute of his driver, and got into a staff car. He gazed around him as he was driven to his meeting in one of the estate houses, which was his regiment's headquarters.

Groups of young men in shorts and vests were running under the watchful eyes of their physical instructors, as others in fatigues, carrying backpacks full of rocks were just completing a fifteen kilometre run.

Things were slowly starting to improve. To begin with the new division had lacked company commanders, platoon leaders and experienced technicians; the severe fighting on the Eastern front had meant heavy casualties in all the divisions and only a few officers and non-commissioned officers had been drafted in to form the nucleus of the new division. Since then they had received forty-three officers from regular army formations, all of whom had been at one time Hitlerjugend leaders. That was the framework.

After the fall of Stalingrad, and with the massive attrition of manpower it had been decided to raise a volunteer division of young men between the age of seventeen and eighteen. There had been some misgivings that such young men would not be able to withstand the physical and mental pressure of modern warfare, but they had proved surprisingly good in their basic training.

Now they were receiving their first contingents of these volunteers, and he was already impressed with their dedication and fierce commitment. Some were already being selected for three-month non-commissioned officers courses, and as a result of much effort, the formations were slowly coalescing into a panzer division.

But there was much still to do, especially in the area of equipment. The panzer artillery regiments in particular were under strength, as were the transport vehicles, but the new Tiger tanks were coming through.

His car pulled up at the house next to the stables, the driver jumped out and opened the door for him.

He went in to yet another urgent planning meeting, making it just before Field Marshal Erwin Rommel's car arrived.

What they needed was time, time to build up their strength, to be ready for the fateful moment when the blow would fall.

As yet nobody knew when that would be.

Inge, along with several other nurses was selected for an important government reception.

They were released in the afternoon and, dressed in their uniforms, they were taken to a ceremonial hall to hear a speech by Herr Goebbels that was to be broadcast to the nation, followed by a reception in which civilian medals were to be awarded for gallantry and service.

The time of four o'clock was significant: American raids would be dying out, the RAF would be yet to come.

They were all in a good mood.

Inge looked at their young faces, thin but bright with life. She was so very proud of them, – working with the constant threat of death, providing an outstanding service to their fellow countrymen.

Inside, the sides of the large hall were lined with swastika flags, adding a sense of pageantry. They took their seats, looking around at the others: workers from the rescue squads, the firemen, the bus drivers and the like, and the police.

The noisy chattering was suddenly hushed as a fanfare of trumpets rang out, played by black-clad SS soldiers, wonderfully smart in their uniforms and steel helmets.

The platform party came on to applause, and then, with another fanfare from the trumpeters the small limping figure of Goebbels in a white uniform, his dark hair brushed straight back, walked up to the podium.

He began in his quiet, fatherly voice, bringing warm greetings and a message from the Führer who was unable to be with them as he was busy leading the planning with his generals, making sure that the might of the Third Reich would fall on their enemies and deliver the final victory.

The struggle for the nation's future demanded a commensurate effort from them all.

He'd barely started when the first of several air raid sirens started wailing.

People shifted uneasily, looking around and at each other as Goebbels continued, until the muffled thunder of the anti-aircraft guns on the flak towers was suddenly punctuated by a sharp crack: bombs.

Everybody started for the shelters, a bleak-looking Goebbels was escorted swiftly from the stage even as an announcer on the state radio was telling the nation that the broadcast was being postponed for technical reasons. But they knew that the sound of the air raid had gone out over the air before they had cut the link.

Down in the shelter the talk was depressing. Were the Americans extending their time, or were the British starting earlier?

They did not know it, but the RAF had heard about the speech through intelligence sources, and had meticulously planned the raid by a force of fast Mosquitos flying beneath the radar. It was intended as a propaganda raid to further depress the morale of the nation, and as such it was working, at least for Inge.

As they sat huddled like frightened sheep in the reinforced concrete shelter, with its dim bulkhead lights, faces that had been so bright and excited were now drawn and worried.

Inge suddenly understood the truth of what Walter had been gently trying to tell her, what, up to now, she had refused to believe: defeat was inevitable in one way or another.

She couldn't imagine that; the Führer would never let that happen.

But their being trapped like rats in a sewer, at a safe time, when they should have been listening to one of the top members of the party, gave her the first intimation that all would *not* be well in the end.

Up to then she had always believed that they would pull through, that Germany would triumph because of the sacrifices and resilience of its people, led by such a wonderful leader.

Now, suddenly, she knew that was not going to happen, that there could not be total victory: it would be something less.

Inge felt a tear rolling down her cheek, and hurriedly brushed it away. She did not want the others to think she was frightened.

But she was.

Not of the bombs.

Not of the enemy.

Not even of death.

But of the future.

# CHAPTER THIRTEEN

They passed over the coast at Southwold with no further incident other than some light flak coming up from barges off the Dutch coast.

Slowly they lost altitude and eventually joined the circuit at Little Staughton.

The landmark spire of the church passed on his left as he was on finals. Lined up with the runway, their wheels touched down with a burst of rubber smoke, at dawn.

Robbie taxied to dispersal. When the engines were turned off the silence was deafening. He went through his checks, then wearily he followed Davey down the short ladder to the concrete below, his legs stiff from sitting for so long.

They were met by a WAAF standing by her Hillman car.

'Nice trip, sir?'

Robbie let Davey do the talking; her eyes were shining with interest for his navigator. He ducked under the aircraft wing, and found a sergeant and a LAC gawping at F-for-Freddie's fuselage. It was peppered with dozens of little holes, but they were looking at something sticking out underneath. He joined them as the sergeant said: 'Cripes, sir, you were bloody lucky.'

An unexploded 88mm flak shell was embedded in the surface. If it had exploded they would have lost their tailplane. Robbie pulled off his flying helmet and ran a hand through his sweat-soaked hair.

They went to the intelligence debriefing and interrogation, holding out their tin mugs for a shot of rum in their hot, stewed tea, before they detailed everything they had seen on the trip and confirming they had reached the target and dropped their flares.

Released, they had a meal, a bath and a shave. Normally he would have crashed out, been asleep in seconds, but he sat in bed, pen and pad ready.

He managed: *My Darling Maddie* ... Davey, coming in from doing his ablutions, paused at the sight of his room-mate, writing pad on his chest, pen still in hand, fast asleep.

Gently he removed the pen, picked up the paper and set them aside on the wooden bedside cabinet, before turning in himself.

They slept, but at airfields all over the east of England nearly 150 beds that had been occupied the day before remained neatly made up.

The men who had slept in them were now either prisoners of war, or dead, having perished by bullet or cannon, been burnt in twisted blackened wreckage, or drowned in the cold waters of the North Sea. Yet others had 'roman candled' to earth, dying where they fell. Some had completely vanished, their very existence ending in a blinding explosion, gone in a twinkling of an eye.

Some had died at the hands of German civilians.

Night after night the war was being taken to the Nazis.

During the day, the Americans took over: Round the clock.

The cost was high.

But Robbie was happy. Before unconsciousness had overtaken him, as he had laid pen to paper, he had been trying to tell her of how he felt after what had happened on their date in London.

He had spent a restless night since he had left her.

Now, he wandered through an awakening London that had never really slept, especially here in Soho. The gutters were full of discarded French letters, mostly near the bombsites. He got completely lost, finding himself in Park Lane with Hyde Park on his left.

There was a mass of anti-aircraft guns and searchlight units; khaki figures everywhere – to-ing and fro-ing from Nissen huts, men and ATS women, carrying their mess tins and towels.

He got into Oxford Street and saw a clock on a huge store that turned out to be Selfridges. He'd left far too early, but thanks to his detour it was nearly time.

He worried about his reception. But *she* had said to come back.

He found the door with its peeling paint and raised the brass doorknocker, which descended with a single loud thud.

The door opened almost immediately.

She was as pretty as a picture, as his father would have said.

And she was *smiling*, eyes alive with warmth.

Breathlessly she said, 'You're right on time.'

Relief flooded through his body with almost physical force. 'You look wonderful.'

Pleased as Punch, she said, 'Thank you,' and plucked at her dress, as though that was what he was talking about.

Her heart was thumping in her ribcage like a trapped wild bird. Maddie knew what it was: the decision taken in the depths of a sleepless night.

She picked up a silk scarf which she proceeded to put round her neck before taking up her trench-style raincoat, dipping one arm in before he took the coat and held it for her as she found the other sleeve.

'Thank you.'

Robbie watched as she buttoned it up, before tying the belt casually around her small waist, leaving the buckle dangling.

'Right, I'm ready. What would you like to do?'

Robbie really didn't care as long as he was with her.

'Well, despite everything, I've never been around London. Perhaps we could see the sights?'

'Very well.'

Somewhere on the way to Buckingham Palace she took his hand when crossing a road, and didn't let go.

Later, as they walked through St James's Park with its ducks, noisy in the spring sunshine, she put her hand through his arm.

He felt ten feet tall.

They stood outside a sandbagged Number Ten Downing Street, standing in a small crowd that remained constant in size as people came and went. He was amazed at the apparent lack of security: just one uniformed bobby wearing a tin hat and carrying a gas mask.

They were turning away when a large black Humber car with a policeman standing on the running board turned in to the cul-de-sac.

A shout went up.

'It's him.'

They ran back and were kept on the opposite pavement by two policemen just holding their arms out. Nobody attempted to press forward.

He was smaller than Robbie had expected; he was wearing a Homburg hat and a grey double-breasted suit, and was smoking a large cigar. He stopped at the entrance to Number Ten, turned briefly towards them and gave his famous 'V' sign. Then he raised his hat, and disappeared through the door.

As they walked away Robbie shook his head in disbelief.

'I never expected to see Churchill in person.'

At the Houses of Parliament he looked up at Big Ben.

'We used to hear the chimes on the wireless at home.'

They strolled on to Westminster Bridge and leant on the parapet, watching dozens of tugs, their long funnels pouring black smoke as they hauled strings of barges up- and downstream, to and from the Pool of London docks.

In the sky above them a number of silver barrage balloons floated gently on their cables. The sun had made the dirty grey water turn to sparkling silver.

He turned and rested his back on the stone balustrade, watching her face as a wisp of hair lifted and fell over her forehead.

He thought it was the most beautiful sight he'd seen in his life.

She lifted her eyes from contemplating the water and looked back at him, smiling shyly as she asked: 'Are you hungry?'

Still jealous of the fact that she knew lots of top brass, he wanted to impress her. Robbie had heard chaps in the mess saying how good the place was. To hell with the cost.

'Yes, let's go to the Savoy Grill. Have you been before?'

Her eyes widened. 'No, but Robbie, the place is frightfully expensive.'

The fact that she hadn't been there before sealed it.

'I don't care. Where is it?'

She giggled. 'Turn round. You've been looking at it.'

He did. She pointed down the curve of the river, past County Hall on their right to a building on the opposite bank straight ahead.

'There, that's the Savoy.'

He grabbed her hand.

'Right – come on.'

# CHAPTER FOURTEEN

At first it seemed pitch black outside, but slowly John Fairfax could see the lightness of the water as the waves lapped on to the pebbles of the harbour area.

She took his hand, led him past the houses, beyond the quay to where the sea ran up on to the sandy beach.

'Where are we going?'

'My place.'

She didn't say anything more.

His heart quickened.

Eventually she led him up a bank of pebbles and on to soft springy turf.

'Here we are.'

He heard a door being opened.

'Wait there while I light the oil lamp – there is no electricity.'

Obediently he stood, wondering what would happen, worried if he would make a fool of himself?

A soft glow suddenly lit up the room. She came to the door.

'Quickly – the blackout.'

He stepped forward, and cracked his head on the lintel.

'Ouch.'

She closed the door.

'You Americans, you are all so tall. Here . . .'

She stood on her toes, stretching up in front of him and began to rub the sore spot with cool fingertips.

It was too much. His hands went round her waist. Immediately hers shot to the back of his head. They kissed, long and hard with a wildness he had never known, until she suddenly broke free. She grabbed his hand and picked up the oil lamp with the other. He allowed himself to be towed to a door to the right of the fireplace, only just remembering to duck as he followed her into the next room.

She turned, eyes twinkling mischievously.

'The cottage is owned by the nuns in Truro.'

An old brass bedstead dominated the bedroom. To the left, above a chest of drawers, was a picture depicting the bleeding heart of Jesus. A very large wooden crucifix dominated the wall above the bed.

When she set the lamp down on the bedside table, Christ in his agony loomed even larger, and a great shadow of the cross ran up the wall and stretched across the ceiling.

The tip of her tongue showed between her teeth before she whispered:

'You're not a Catholic are you?'

He woke in the morning to find the rays of sunlight from the small window falling upon his face. She stirred beside him, pushing her warm naked back up against his chest. He felt her sweet-smelling hair beneath his face.

She turned, wrapped her arms around him, pressed her soft firm breasts into his chest and gave him a dreamy look.

'I suppose you'll want your breakfast?'

He did.

They decided to walk to the next village. It was low tide, but the rolling Atlantic waves were breaking further out, the green-blue water giving way to foaming white as they thundered on to the beach.

They passed a towering cliff and walked on into the next bay, with another rocky headland beyond.

A fine spray drifted inland, seen only against the darkness of the cliffs, but they could taste the salt on their lips.

Outdoors, among these hills, cliffs and beaches, with her, he felt the happiest he'd ever been.

On their return, the tide was coming in fast. She pointed at the last headland before the cottage.

'Oops, the sea is already up to the rocks.'

He shrugged. 'OK, let's paddle around it.'

Sally laughed.

'Right-ho, tough guy.'

He sat on a rock, took off his boots and socks, and tied them around his neck.

She wasn't wearing stockings, so she just kicked off her shoes. She swept her dress up and tucked it into her knickers.

'What are you doing that for?'

She nodded at the sea.

'You'll be up to your knees, and it's rough, so it will splash.'

He looked at the waves and realized she was right. In a couple of moments he had taken off his trousers and was standing there in his shorts.

'Come on, then.'

Hand in hand they waded into the water. It was viciously cold.

He yelled out 'Jeesus,' then knew his mother would have been horrified and let go of her hand.

'I thought it was supposed to be the Atlantic, not the Arctic Ocean?'

She laughed and carried on.

He followed her, taken by the fact that she looked like a little girl with her dress up, her white legs seeming even whiter as the sea surged around them. The cold in his own legs was such that he started to run, splashing her as he passed.

She screamed, 'You beast!' and followed him. It developed into a race, until he stubbed his toe on a submerged rock and fell flat on to his face, the salt water going up his nose.

Choking, he stood up, but she was pointing and laughing. He turned, to see his trousers disappearing under another wave.

By the time he'd recovered them he was blue with cold.

Back in the cottage she helped him out of his wet things, towelling his lower parts as, shaking with the cold, he did his own head and shoulders.

She felt a sense of propriety and, strangely, rather like a mother attending her child. His manhood, which had given her so much pleasure, but held her in subjugation to his maleness, was now small and defenceless.

The lot of women, she thought: lover, mother, and ultimately nurse.

After supper he got the galvanized bath off the hook outside the back door and put it in front of the hearth. Sally was heating the water in buckets on the range, which was burning brightly.

While they waited they played records, he cranking the handle and bringing the arm gently down until the needle touched the gently undulating black surface of the shellac.

There were old music hall numbers, vaudeville as he called it, others were Irish ballads sung by John McCormack. One special one caught his eye – 'Softly Falls the Moonlight' sung by the once famous opera diva, Adelina Patti. It was a favourite of his mother's: she had a version of it in her Christy Minstrels songbook. He played it several times, then remembered that moonlight might soon be less than romantic for him: dangerous moonlight.

There were a few records from the twenties, and some rather more recent ones: soft tenor voices crooning with smooth understated saxophones playing foxtrots and quicksteps. He wondered why the nuns had them, but Sally thought they'd probably been left by other guests. They danced, shuffling on the wooden floor in a corner, sometimes still dreamily together as the needle clicked endlessly at the end of the record.

It took an hour for the water to boil. She went first, holding his hand as she stepped delicately into the water. By the glow of the oil lamp he lovingly bathed her slim exposed neck, her hair tied up, the soapy water sliding down over her slim shoulders and pink-tipped breasts.

He went next. Sally, kneeling beside him, gently washed his broad back, kissing his neck and shoulder as she did so.

They made love on the couch before the fire. In the soft warm glow of the oil lamp and the flickering light of the fire, she seemed to him like some wonderful creature who had appeared from the very earth of this extraordinary, magical place.

# CHAPTER FIFTEEN

Walter Raus was also by the sea, looking out across the Channel through huge mounted binoculars. His view was of white cliffs and a pebble beach with rolls of barbed wire winding into the distance.

He could see the khaki-clad Tommies patrolling along the cliff-tops.

Walter thought back to the last time he had been here. It had been in 1940, as a very junior officer, a SS Untersturmführer.

Then, despite their jubilation at the great victory, they had argued bitterly amongst themselves as to why Hitler had held them back for the vital hours that had allowed the British to evacuate their army from the beaches at Dunkirk.

Later, the word in the mess, from above, was that Hitler had tried to conclude a separate peace with Britain. He regarded the British as members of the Germanic race.

However, all of them agreed that he had completely misjudged Churchill who, they gathered from the news bulletins, was determined to destroy National Socialism and Hitler.

They all knew that since those heady days the British had been steadily replacing their losses, and that there had also been a terrific build-up of the American forces in England, despite the heavy damage inflicted by the U-boats; his brother would attest to that.

At the thought of his brother he frowned. Apparently there had been no communication with his boat for over two months now. Naval headquarters said this was not unusual, but the family were not convinced. He made a mental note to ask Inge to get in touch with his sister-in-law.

His attention returned to the scene before him. Through the magnifying lenses the waves breaking at the foot of the cliffs were clearly quite rough, despite the sunny day. He might have been landing there back in 1940.

Everybody had been relieved when Operation Sea Lion was cancelled. For several wearisome months they had practised loading and unloading from barges and one or two specialized ships, mostly under simulated battle conditions.

And all the while the Luftwaffe was losing the battle for air superiority over Britain, and without it, they could not risk the crossing whilst the British Navy with its capital ships would be able to intervene. It would have been slaughter.

He stepped back, down off the metal step and paced further along the rampart of the huge concrete gun emplacement set in the hillside.

There might still be a lot to do, but they were in much better shape than the British had been, except. . . .

As if to underline his concern a flight of nine fighter aircraft thundered in low overhead, the roundels on their wings clearly showing they were RAF.

He watched as they dwindled into the distance inland.

There were still air battles, but the Luftwaffe was losing again. This time over their own territory.

Field Marshal Erwin Rommel had made it known in all his briefings that he knew full well the awesome might of the enemy airforce. It had led him to quarrel with Marshal Gerd von Rundstedt, and even the Führer.

Rommel wanted the panzer divisions close to the coast to reduce the aerial threat to their deployment. He knew it was essential that the enemy had to be stopped at the water's edge.

All to no avail. Hitler had insisted they be held inland in reserve.

Walter grunted. He could also appreciate that they had to be ready to reinforce anywhere on 3,000 miles of coastline. It was a dilemma.

On the way back to the divisional headquarters his driver was stopped by military police at a crossroads. A police corporal saluted as he came forward and explained his action to Walter.

'We have cornered French terrorists in a farmhouse about three kilometres down the road, sir. There is going to be an attack.'

Walter nodded. 'I see – and the detour?'

The corporal pointed. 'It's all clearly marked, sir, takes you through the village and then back on to this road.'

Walter raised his hand to his cap in a languid salute to show that he understood.

The corporal stepped back, snapped a crisp 'Heil Hitler', then waved the driver on.

It was early spring, and the fields and hills of the French countryside looked clean and fresh and full of bursting life.

As the car lumbered along the road, Walter leant his head back, looked up at the sun flickering through the new leaves.

It reminded him of the first time he had taken Inge on a week's holiday to Berlin, before they were married. They had had the full approval of both families, and everything was very correct with Inge in one hotel, he in another.

On their first day, hand in hand, they had explored the still bomb-free city, doing nothing special, just talking and revelling in each other's company, getting to know more about their likes and dislikes as the days went past. They'd strolled with other Berliners in the Tiergarten, standing before the statue of the Empress Auguste Viktoria as they enjoyed Italian ice cream, and on another day poking fun at Hercules on the Liechtenstein Bridge, and then looking down at the colourful barges on the landwenkanal.

But more than anything the dappled light coming through the trees evoked the memory of their favourite café on the Potsdamer Platz, sipping real coffee and watching the world go by.

It seemed a long time ago now, almost as though it were somebody else's lifetime.

The car jolted in a pothole, bringing him out of his reverie. He raised his head. They'd begun to go through the village.

He looked around at the quaint, mellow, old stone-built houses and shops. In the tree-lined square in the centre a fruit and vegetable market was in progress.

As the car rumbled down the cobblestones on one side of the square they passed a church, then turned the corner.

Before them was a little café with tables and chairs, crowded with shoppers and several Wehrmacht officers.

'Stop here,' Walter ordered.

He alighted and pulled off his vulcanized coat. Tugging his uniform jacket into smarter shape, he said: 'I'm going to have something to eat. Do what you wish. Be back here in an hour.'

He found a table and sat with his back to a wall.

When the white-aproned waiter came he ordered a plate of *moules marinières* and a bottle of local red wine.

He looked around, enjoying the scene, the normality of it all. Voices carried, he could hear the sounds of girls' laughter and the clip-clop noise made by the wooden shoes of some of the country people on the cobbles.

The waiter returned, and presented his bottle with its label. After the cork was drawn and Walter had sniffed and tasted the swirling ruby-red liquid he nodded his assent, and the waiter poured more into the glass.

Walter drank a little, savouring its rough but honest simplicity – he grinned inwardly at his analysis.

It was just like being on holiday. After all that he had experienced in Russia, and thinking of Inge and the bombing in Berlin, it was so wonderfully peaceful. If only she could be with him and they could live together in a time of peace.

And then, as his *moules* arrived, there came the sound of automatic gunfire and the boom of something heavier: mortars. The counter-attack on the Maquis had started.

Immediately the atmosphere changed. The crowd thinned. Several people got up from their tables and left, their eyes at the best vacant, unseeing, at the worst, cold, hostile. Especially to him. He was the only one in the black uniform, with lightning bolts on his collar: the SS symbol.

The relaxed holiday mood was gone.

It was back to the harsh reality of the time.

A time of war.

# CHAPTER SIXTEEN

When Robbie woke up it was to find a LAC shaking him gently by the shoulder.

'Sir, sir. The CO wants a word, sir, says it's urgent.'

Robbie stumbled into his clothes, did a quick shave, his braces down around his hips. It took him all of fifteen minutes to get presentable and dash over to the office.

Puzzled, he was ushered before the squadron CO, who was sitting behind his desk and who answered his salute by saying: 'Sit down Robbie. I've got some rather unsettling news.'

Robbie felt his heart miss a beat.

'Is it my mother or father, sir? Are they all right?' Then he immediately thought of Maddie.

'It's not Miss Hayes, is it?'

The CO gave him a rather disparaging look.

'No, no, calm down. It's just, well, you've been given an urgent posting – away from the squadron.'

Robbie's face dropped. All he could manage was: 'But why?'

The CO shuffled some papers. 'You're being sent to a new Typhoon squadron – part of the Second Tactical Airforce. With the second front coming there's an urgent need for fighter-bomber pilots to do close work with the army – hell of a rush, so I've got a feeling the big day ain't that far away. Anyway, sorry to see you go.'

He stood up, held out his hand.

'You've been a good man to have on the squadron, Robbie. We'll miss you. Best of luck. Your movement orders are with the adjutant.' The squadron leader gave a knowing wink. 'With a forty-eight hour pass for you before you report to Milfield, so if you get going you'll be able to squeeze in a visit to that Miss Hayes.'

Robbie stood, saluted, and left in some confusion.

Less than two hours later he was on a train from Sandy to Kings Cross, looking out at the smoke from the engine drifting out across the fields, not seeing anything, thinking only of what had happened the last time he was in London.

Despite her misgivings, they had ended up in the Grill Room of the Savoy, along with, it seemed to him, half the American Expeditionary Force.

When they got back to her place in the late afternoon, and climbed the creaking stairs once more, the sun had long gone from her rooms.

'That was wonderful, Robbie. Thank you again, the food was out of this world.'

With his hand he indicated that it was nothing, he'd enjoyed every minute of it, even though one of his 'emergency' white fivers from the back of his wallet was now missing. The meal was five shillings each – the maximum that was allowed, but a rash purchase of a bottle of wine – a luxury – had done the damage.

She made for the kitchen.

'Put your feet up while I make us a nice pot of tea.'

He did, and closed his eyes. When she returned with a tray he was fast asleep. Quietly Maddie put it down, and carefully sat, noiselessly pushing off her shoes and curling her legs up beneath her. For a long time she studied him as he lay before her. In his sleep he looked even more innocent and young.

But her eyes fell to his tunic, not to the white wings on his blue-uniformed chest but to the strips of coloured ribbon. Other than that they represented medals she did not know what they were for, but they did remind her that he was, night after night, in danger, fighting a war, risking death.

It didn't bear thinking about. Her own eyes felt heavy. She closed them for a moment. It seemed like only seconds, but she came to with a start, realizing that she too had been asleep.

It was then that she became conscious of his eyes on her.

They looked at each other for several seconds, until she blinked.

'How long have you been awake?'

'Maybe five minutes.'

She straightened up and put the fingers of one hand to her forehead, pressing at the skin where a faint niggle had started.

'I hope I didn't have my mouth open?'

He grinned. 'No, it was closed.'

She raised an eyebrow. 'You should have woken me up.'

'Why? You looked so beautiful.' He blushed at his frankness.

Robbie slowly stood up, began buttoning his jacket.

'I've had a wonderful day.'

Surprised, she shot to her feet.

'You're not going, are you?'

He hesitated. 'You must be tired. . . .'

She shook her head. 'Not at all. Wouldn't you like to do something this evening?'

Robbie was delighted; he had been fearing that the day had finished.

'Have you anything in mind?'

'We could see if we could get into a show.'

London nightlife was getting under way as they hopped on a bus. When they got to a theatre it was to find it crowded outside, and full on the inside. They took another bus – but the next one was sold out too.

'Let's go for a drink instead, we're never going to get in anywhere.'

She was holding on to his arm, already pulling him gently in the direction of a corner pub.

He found a seat for her, and left her chatting to an older woman with a fox fur over her shoulders, the face of the animal looking malevolently out through the cigarette smoke at the women's glass of stout.

When he came back with their drinks it seemed as if the fox spoke in a low gravelly voice.

'This yer young man, then?'

Embarrassed, Robbie looked at the woman, then Maddie raised an eyebrow and smiled. 'I suppose so.'

Robbie knew his face had gone the colour of a brick.

When they got back to her door he didn't know what to expect, but she said, 'Quickly,' as she held it open and ushered him inside.

'I really ought to be going.'

As soon as the door closed she reached up, put her hands around the back of his head – and drew him down on to her lips.

This time it was very gentle, the merest brush.

When they parted she took him by the hand and led him upstairs.

At the top he eventually managed: 'Maddie, I. . . .'

She pushed him firmly down on to the sofa, and put a finger to his lips.

'Wait here.'

She disappeared into the bedroom, closed the door and sat down on the edge of the bed, her heart pounding. Maddie had thought about what she intended to do all night and all day, and at last the moment had come.

Since she was seven years old the piano had dominated her life, virtually to the exclusion of everything else, especially in the last few years.

While she had been burning with a feverish desire to excel in the one area of her life that had any meaning, there had also been another, darker side to her hours and hours of practice after normal school with Sister Bridget.

Her father, after the last war, had never been able to settle down again, and had 'taken to the drink'.

The family had sunk into poverty, and with it had come violence. Her mother dreaded the sound of her husband's arrival at the front door after an evening of drinking away what little income they had. On a good evening it was just his tongue, on a bad one. . . .

Sometimes her mother had had to go to the doctor and tell lies about the cause of her injuries. The doctor became suspicious and eventually had a word with the police and the local priest, but nothing ever came of it. They all seemed to be indifferent, as if it was something that was a part of a married woman's life and had to be endured.

When, aged fifteen, she had tried to defend her mother, Maddie had been savagely beaten with his belt.

She began to realize that her presence, the plaudits and success she was getting, seemed to be making him worse, as though he was jealous.

And she was uncomfortably aware, as her breasts grew, of the way he looked at her.

Near the end, in the last few months while she was awaiting the scholarship decision, she wondered whether she was ever going to be able to get away.

He'd made it plain he wanted her to stay, and in one drunken rage had even held her hand on the table, holding a hammer raised with his other arm, and threatened to smash it, before her mother had taken a carving knife from a drawer and screamed she would kill him.

Thankfully it had worked, though it had cost her mother a backhander that had taken away a tooth.

So there had been no boyfriends in her life, not even now amongst the handsome, fit young men who crowded around her piano, or with whom, in a group, she went to social occasions in a London that was living on the edge.

There was always a barrier: her fear and distrust of men. She lived for one thing: her music, above all her music.

So what she was about to do made no sense.

But then, nothing made sense any more.

The door opened.

Maddie stood in her thin nightdress, her hair loosened. Modestly she held her two hands joined together in front of her, head down, like a little girl.

She whispered, 'Robbie, you should know . . . I've never done this before.'

He stood up, swallowed hard.

'Neither have I.'

# CHAPTER SEVENTEEN

The days passed, and John Fairfax never once thought of the world outside their own existence, until that world intruded on theirs. The first time it happened they'd been for another long walk, were back on their beach as out at sea clouds were building again, great towering shapes that curled and changed on their surface in a turmoil that hinted at the natural forces within.

Sally went home to put the kettle on as he scouted for some more firewood. He came across a crate lid. It turned out to be bigger than he expected, half-buried in the pebble bank.

As he struggled to free it he saw the name of a company stencilled on its top. It was the Baltimore Precision Tool Corp.

He knew then that it was more than likely from a torpedoed ship bringing supplies across the Atlantic, from the 'Arsenal of Democracy' as Roosevelt had styled America.

He wondered how many men had drowned in the icy seas, or burnt to death in the inferno of oil-covered water, doing their duty.

It reminded him of why he was standing there, thousands of miles from home, and of the job he had trained to do – had still to do: his duty.

And Betty – his duty to her. Sadly, he would write as soon as he had returned from leave. It would not be easy.

Moments later the storm broke in all its North Atlantic fury, the wild sea breaking in huge explosions of white water that erupted up the granite rock faces that marked the very edge of Europe.

He was halfway up the darkening beach when the first few drops of rain hit him, coldly smacking on to his skin.

Inside the cottage, the drumming of the rain on the roof and windows, and the distant booming of the watery detonations, followed by a faint vibration of the floor, brought home the raw strength of nature.

While Sally busied herself in the scullery with the food he turned his attention to the fire, which had gone out. He raked the ashes with a poker through the bars, then tore some old newspapers into sheets, twisting them up into 'sticks' as she had instructed. He placed them in the grate, added a layer of kindling from splintered boxwood, and applied a match. As soon as it was well alight, snapping and flaring, he added some larger pieces of wood, and a couple of lumps of coal.

Unknown to him, Sally was standing in the scullery doorway lovingly watching him on his knees before the grate. She felt a sudden stab of sadness. Another day and he would be gone back to wherever he was stationed. Back to the bloody, bloody war. She didn't know whether she could survive another loss.

After David she had nearly given up on life. They had talked so much about their wedding day, argued light-heartedly over the number of children they would have, dreamed of little things like what they would grow in the garden, and joked about themselves in old age.

There never had been a proper funeral, he'd gone down in the Channel. He had, in effect, just disappeared from her life.

What had stopped her from ending it all she did not know, but one day she had got up in the morning, given the wedding dress to the Salvation Army and joined the WRNS.

In her spare time, using a torch under the bedclothes after lights out, she had started to jot down a few lines, of the way she felt, of what she observed in others.

Now the first slim notebook was full and she was on a second, with an idea that one day she might write a book. The fanciful title that she had just printed on the cover was 'Softly Falls The Moonlight', after the old record he kept playing.

They had known each other for only days, not yet a week, but. . . .

If anything happened to him she had no idea whether she would survive this time.

She felt the heat come into her eyes.

He turned, found her staring at him, tears flowing down her cheeks. He didn't have to ask what the matter was; he just got up, crossed to her, and wrapped his arms around her as her body convulsed with great sobs.

He stroked her hair, kissed the top of her head, and soothed her with words as he might do with a little girl: a daughter, if he had one.

Gently he got her to the sofa, sat down with her, gave her his handkerchief as she wiped her eyes and blew her nose.

'What must you think of me?'

He smiled. 'I think everything of you. Will you marry me?'

It just came out.

Sally just stared at him, until his anxious face made her whisper:

'It's been nearly a week,' – she gave a weak smile, 'I thought you'd never ask.'

Relieved, he nevertheless had to hear her answer.

'Well?'

'Of course I will.'

Neither of them ever thought for a moment about how little time they had known each other. Neither of them had been so instantly sure about anything in their lives before.

They spent the afternoon on the sofa, just talking. Not even the sound of hailstones battering on the window, the moaning of the wind in the eaves, or the steady roar of the distant surf disturbed their dreams, their plans for the future.

After the wreckage on the beach the second intrusion came on their last evening. They walked on the top of the cliffs, he with an arm over her shoulders, she with an arm round his waist, watching the seabirds effortlessly swooping and soaring against the backdrop of cliffs and breakers, gannets suddenly folding their wings and dropping straight as an arrow into the sea, emerging with wriggling fish in their beaks.

The wind was gusting again, white horses were peppering the grey waters. They reached a narrow, steep pathway leading down to a little cove, and half-slithered, half-climbed down to the rocky shore.

In a sheltered corner, on a flat sea-polished rock they sat down. He got out his cigarettes and lit up for both of them, passing one to her.

For a while they sat quietly watching the majesty of nature all around them until he said: 'It's like being at the end of the world.'

Gravely she agreed.

'Yes, all alone with you – how ghastly.'

Chuckling, he gave her a nudge, which she returned, and like a couple of giggling kids they kept doing it until he pretended to fall off the end of the rock.

She held out her hand and helped to haul him on to an even keel.

He finished his cigarette and flicked the butt into a pool surrounded by dense banks of bladderwrack seaweed, where it died with a hiss.

Sally was still smoking hers, and looked at the tip as she quietly said:

'When will I be able to see you again?'

It was the question he had been dreading. He knew that his chance of more leave in the next few months was remote. From his assessment of their training, and recently its increased tempo, the day of destiny couldn't be far away.

He compressed his lips, shook his head.

'I don't know.' He brightened. 'What if you got stationed near me? I can get out most weekends.'

She frowned. 'It might be possible. I'll look into it, see if it might be arranged on compassionate grounds if we were married.'

Smiling, he nodded. 'Sooner the better.'

They talked more, planning about what they could, or could not do, until one of the waves threw up a higher spray as it hit a rock.

'Tide's coming in.'

She pressed the end of her cigarette against the rock surface, before taking both of his hands as he hauled her to her feet.

They scrambled back up the path, he sometimes pushing her bottom to help her up the steeper parts.

She slapped his hand away, giggled.

'Now that you plan to make an honest woman of me all that hanky-panky will have to stop.'

'Oh yeah?'

He grabbed hold of her. It seemed appropriate that they should make love out there, in the wildness of the Cornish country where they had met.

They had finished eating and, were washing the plates in the scullery when a muffled explosion sent them rushing to the door. He stood with his arm protectively around her as more thumps reached their ears, and searchlights flickered on the horizon. She trembled slightly.

He asked: 'What is it?'

She frowned. 'Probably E-boats attacking a convoy.'

A long string of explosions, one after the other, followed.

Sally shook her head. 'No, that sounded like depth charges. Perhaps they've cornered a U-boat.'

It lasted for an hour, then they were left with the sound of the waves gently falling on the beach, and the dragging noise of pebbles pulled back by the retreating water.

He wondered what the outcome had been. Enemy or not, he shuddered at the thought of men dying in the blackness of their iron tomb.

The spell had been broken.

Into the peace and tranquillity of their little bit of heaven, the titanic struggle that was going on for Europe had at last intruded.

Next morning he appeared from the bedroom dressed in his uniform.

It was the first time she had seen it on him. When he'd moved from the pub he'd brought it in his bag.

He could see from the look on her face that she was upset.

'Sorry.'

She crossed to him, straightened his collar, dusted his shoulders, and then slid her arms around him, face against his chest.

'Take care, you will take care, won't you?'

Into her sweet-smelling hair he promised, knowing, as he did, that he could promise nothing.

What would be would be.

# CHAPTER EIGHTEEN

Inge was shocked.

She'd only just started her shift when there came a commotion from the direction of the staff toilets: screaming – a woman. She joined the rush to help, and found it was a girl she was friendly with; she had started in nursing school with her.

Anna Müller was sprawled on the floor, blood all over her legs and uniform. And in the lavatory bowl was a foetus.

That was disturbing enough, but frankly, miscarriages were very common, especially after heavy bombing attacks, or following dreadful personal news from the front.

It was not the miscarriage that had shocked her. They had tidied everything up, and Inge personally had taken care of Anna, getting her into one of the bunk beds the nurses had in their rest room; her friend's face was as white as the pillow on which her head lay.

Inge got on with her work, checking on Anna occasionally, and was pleased to see a tinge of pink come back into her cheeks.

Then the American bombers came. It was not quite as heavy a raid as usual, and not particularly close. She took a nervous patient with a bad heart condition in a wheelchair from the cardiac clinic to the basement. They had only been there about twenty minutes when the all-clear sounded and the hospital air raid warden said they could return to their duties.

She left the clinic at midday, returned to the ward and reported to Sister, who said she could take her lunch break then.

On her way out she popped in to check on Anna and found her sobbing her heart out, her small defeated body racked with convulsions.

Inge sat down, put her arms around her, held on tight, stroking her friend's hair and rocking gently with her.

Eventually she found out what was the matter. Another nurse, a Nazi Party worker had reported her as having had an abortion. Under the Nazis, abortions on Aryan women were strictly forbidden.

Anna wailed, 'But Inge, we so wanted this baby. How could she?'

Inge could only guess at the reason, probably jealousy or something else. Anna fought back a sob. 'I have to go before a tribunal. I could go to prison for nine months.'

She burst into tears again.

Inge carried on comforting her, but her own head was full of dreadful thoughts. She and Walter had made love without any 'Parisian's' protection – not only because they wanted babies, but in any case they were difficult to get and expensive, even for an SS officer.

So far nothing had happened, though this month her period was late; but that could be down to so many things.

What shocked her was that anyone would make such an accusation against Anna, whose husband was the holder of an Iron Cross. He had been severely wounded, and was lucky to have got out from Stalingrad at all.

She doubted whether the party worker – or family – who had 'smeared' her friend had given so much to the Reich.

And what if Inge miscarried?

That she was known to be a friend of Anna might put her in danger too.

The social framework was beginning to unravel; everybody was becoming suspicious and wary of everybody else. Perhaps it had always been like that, but she had not been aware of it before. They were living in terrible times.

And trying to bring in new life.

Was it right?

# CHAPTER NINETEEN

'What would you like for breakfast?' Maddie called out to Robbie. He was in the tiny room outside her landing door, putting a stopper in the basin.

He yelled back, 'I don't want to take your rations.'

When the basin was full he started soaping up his face.

He called out again. 'I've got a better idea. Why don't you let me treat you to breakfast?'

She appeared in the doorway, clasping her hands around a mug of steaming Camp coffee. Despite the cold he was stark naked. She glanced suggestively at his, what she had heard other girls call 'wedding tackle', that had left her so bruised but happy.

She was still staggered at how quickly they had lost their physical shyness. Now it was as if they'd been married for ever.

Had her mother known such happiness once? For a moment it made her intensely sad, then she snapped out of it.

'All right.'

She gave him a quick peck on his soapy cheek.

'After what you've done to me you can jolly well fork out for breakfast.'

He shouted after her. 'And for what I'm going to do.'

They went to Lyons Corner House, had powdered-egg omelette and one strip of bacon each. The bread was a grey colour, and tasteless.

Over a refreshed pot of weak tea he offered her a cigarette from his packet of Players.

She took one, waiting for him to light her up.

They both breathed out smoke. He wanted to know something straight away.

Mournfully he asked, 'Have you got to go into college today?'

'I'll say I was sick. Doctor Pedlow will give me a note – he's a sweetie.'

Robbie brightened, 'You sure? I wouldn't want to get in the way of your music?'

Maddie smiled at his genuine concern.

'Don't worry, I'll catch up.' Her eyes twinkled. 'If you really don't want to interfere with my musical career—'

'No, of course not.'

'Then let's go for a picnic this lunchtime.'

Bewildered, he looked out of the window. The weather was rather overcast and it was trying to rain. He pulled his chin into his chest.

'What – today?'

She smiled over the rim of the cup she was holding with two hands.

'Don't worry. Not outside. Have you heard of Dame Myra Hess?'

He nodded. 'She does those concerts at the National Gallery, doesn't she?'

'That's right. She played throughout the blitz. People love her.'

Robbie took in her face; her eyes were alive with enthusiasm as she spoke, and he knew where they were going to for lunch.

'But I don't understand the picnic bit.'

She explained. 'The long galleries have had all the priceless works of art taken to safety, so during her recitals people take food and drink in with them.'

'Right, let's do that.'

But she detected a trace of disappointment in his voice.

'Did you have something else in mind?'

He shrugged. 'Just that sometime I wouldn't mind seeing St Paul's Cathedral.'

Maddie jumped up. 'Come on. We can do both. We'll get a taxi – my treat. I insist.'

As they got near to St Paul's he could see that the bombing had been worse in the east of London, with whole blocks of buildings gone. But there, amidst all the ruins, standing defiantly, was Wren's great cathedral. Somehow it seemed to sum up the nations spirit.

He wondered whether there was some building in Berlin that the Germans thought of in the same way?

Half an hour later they went up the steps of the National Gallery, past the sandbagged entrancep; behind them was Trafalgar Square where Nelson stood on top of his column.

Inside there were rows of already occupied wooden chairs facing a grand piano beneath the cupola. Most of the audience were in uniform. Robbie and Maddie walked past them and turned into a long viewing gallery. People were already laying out tablecloths on the wooden floor, and setting out their 'picnics'.

Maddie had barely got their food spread out when the sound of clapping announced the arrival of Dame Myra Hess.

'Is she German?' Robbie asked, remembering the poster outside depicting a well-made lady with dark hair and a prominent nose.

Maddie snorted. 'No, she was born in London. I'm studying her technique – she's brilliant.'

Robbie looked at her and grinned.

'Sorry.'

She winced. 'No – I'm sorry. I get so carried away sometimes.'

An expectant hush fell, then the first notes of a Mozart piano sonata echoed around the building.

Robbie watched Maddie as, eyes closed, she lost herself in the music that a man from Saltzburg – a city now in the Third Reich since the Anschluss – had composed in another, equally turbulent age.

In the interval she handed out the spam sandwiches she had made, as he poured glasses of Tizer for them both.

Anxiously she asked: 'Are you enjoying it?'

Maddie was worried that she'd been selfish, but Robbie leant forward and gave her a peck on the cheek, dispelling the little frown as he said: 'Of course I am. I feel I'm sharing in your life.'

Relieved, she put her hand over his.

'That's what I want. Robbie, I've never brought anyone here before. I want you to understand that.'

She searched his face, was happy when he nodded.

There was nothing else to say. Both knew that something deeper was happening.

He decided he'd better start writing home to tell them about her, how he felt, and that he wanted to marry her as soon as possible.

It seemed crazy but he knew that was what he wanted. He'd never been more sure of anything in his life before.

After the interval the second half commenced with Chopin's polonaise: 'The Heroic'.

Her warm breath played in his ear as she whispered: 'They played this over and over again on Radio Warsaw until, abruptly, it stopped. Everybody knew then that the city had fallen.'

She leant back against the wall, sitting with her legs gracefully to one side, her eyes closed as she concentrated on the music.

He took in every lovable detail of her and wondered, should he pop the question now, before he went back?

But he knew that when Germany was finished he would be sent to the Far East to fight the Japanese.

For the first time he began personally to hate the war.

# CHAPTER TWENTY

The next month for John Fairfax was one of non-stop hard training. Every day the tension was ratcheted up a little, and all of Southern England was now one huge army camp, with over three million men, training – and waiting.

He'd written to Sally straight away, and at the first opportunity had gone to see the adjutant to request further leave.

The adjutant had looked up at him through his rimless glasses, which caught the light from the shadeless bulb in the ceiling.

'Hardly likely, son, but put it into writing and stress any points that might make the difference.'

The adjutant scowled, his glasses flashing again as he'd turned his attention back to the writing on his desk. 'But in case you hadn't noticed, there is a war to be won.'

That hurt. He was in a crack all-volunteer force, and it looked like he was taking his eye off the ball.

But there was no accounting for the chance meeting with Sally Dytham, a woman who had changed everything – for ever.

'But sir, it's because I wish to marry an English girl – before we see action.'

The adjutant paused, removed his glasses and slowly shook his head.

'The CO won't give permission son, not after all the failed marriages of the doughboys in the last war. He's turned down quite a few already; it's official policy.'

His words were a crushing blow to John Fairfax.

But there was no time to brood over the disappointment, as the training became more specific to the role they would play on that fateful day when the time came to break Hitler's Atlantic Wall.

Just before he climbed into a truck forming part of a huge convoy that was to take them to Torquay for an exercise code named Tiger, he received three letters from the mail corporal.

He pushed them into one of his baggy trouser pockets and buttoned the flap, but not before recognizing the two airmails from home. One was with Sis's handwriting, the other was from Betty. The third letter had a Penzance postmark.

Whistles were blowing and the lead trucks were moving out. He clambered up into the cab's passenger seat.

When they reached Torquay on the south coast he found that they were quartered in a seafront hotel. Having made sure his men were settled in, he found a quiet corner and hunched down against a wall.

He fished out the letters. He had meant to save hers to the last, but found his eager hands tearing at it before he could stop himself. He noticed it had been opened and resealed with the army censor's stamp.

He took out the two sheets of fine notepaper, not realizing they were pre-war, and immediately smelt her perfume.

He unfolded them and started reading.

*My darling John, I miss you so desperately, it's like a great big hole in my heart. I miss your arms around me, your breath on my body, your taste, the sound of your voice – I could go on for ever.*

*I've walked our beaches every day, but without you it's not the same. But I've got some good news – in that I've been in touch with my CO, and am going back tomorrow with a view to getting a transfer on compassionate grounds to a WREN unit on the south coast. I mentioned our intention to marry. I know it's not as near as you would like, but darling, I will be much better placed to come up and see you, perhaps even on day trips?*

She ended with:

*I'm already packed, and a farmer is giving me a lift into Penzance first thing in the morning.*

*Darling, I'm writing this letter in front of the fire, wishing you were here beside me. Later, I will lie in our bed and listen to the waves, looking through the window at the stars twinkling above the unseen ocean, knowing those stars are looking down on you too.*

*Goodnight my love, take good care of yourself for me and please John, make it so we can meet soon, I'm lost without you.*

She signed it *Sally*, and there was the outline of her lips: she'd used some of her precious lipstick on them and pressed them to the paper.

He held the letter to his own lips before folding it back into the envelope and putting it carefully into a top pocket. How the hell was he going to tell her what the adjutant had said?

Reluctantly, and not without a rush of guilt, he opened Betty's letter.

She told him about things happening back home in the good old US of A, and about people he knew, where they were, what they were doing and, saddest of all, that two of their college friends had died fighting in the Pacific at Guadalcanal.

She had put kiss crosses on the bottom of the sheet. Feeling wretched, he put it into his trouser pocket – not next to Sally's.

Sis's letter was full of fun, made him smile, until he reached the last paragraph, and read:

*By the way, saw Betty's mother in town today, she says she's in the Army Nursing Corps and nearly finished her four week training course for newly commissioned nurses – but I expect she's written you with all that.*

*It sounded very intensive to me. Her mother prattled on about learning to defend against mechanized attack, gas and chemicals, field sanitation – god she did go on.*

*Anyway, got to sign off big brother, you take care of yourself now, no volunteering eh? Who knows, Betty may end up at a field hospital near you soon – great eh!*

*All my love, Jennifer.*

He lowered the letter, shocked.

He hadn't known that she'd left the Red Cross to train as an army nurse. Keeping it a secret was not like her. There'd never been a mention of it in her letters. He worried for her, aware that army nurses had been under fire, and had sustained casualties in Sicily and Salerno.

The next day they were back in the trucks that were substituting for the C-47 transport aircraft, the men joking that it was rougher on them as they bounced down English lanes full of potholes than if they'd been in the air.

They were ordered out at an area behind Slapton Sands, a big wide bay of fine yellow sand rising gently to a coast road.

He slept in a field with his men until midnight, when the trucks were used again, bringing them to the area that was the supposed drop zone – apparently by moonlight. To the south, out in the channel, great flashes, soundless, lit up the sky.

When they were all sorted out he led them, with the rest of the battalion, marching through a mist to a raised point about a mile back from the beach at Slapton Sands. They arrived as dawn broke in the eastern sky.

The men gasped in amazement at the huge fleet of amphibious assault craft and larger transport ships covering the entire bay before them. It was obviously a rehearsal for the main landings.

'Come on, come on.' He clapped his hands together. 'Start digging.'

They set up a defensive position, and then waited until the first troops of the 4th Infantry started passing their position.

They seemed in an ugly mood, sweating with their loads of equipment, panting and cursing.

Later, he and all the other junior officers were briefed that on no account were they to talk or write about the exercise to anyone, and that they were to go back to their companies and platoons and inform their men of the same. It was emphasized that this was very important.

He'd never seen such glum, serious faces before. Surely it wasn't all that bad? Had something terrible happened? Later in the day rumours started to circulate. Scores of bodies of American soldiers had washed up on the beaches of southern England. An 'E-boat' had got among the landing craft on the exercise, with terrible results.

As soon as he had showered he lay on his cot and began to write to her.

He told her that he loved her even more, if that was possible, that indeed absence did make his heart grow fonder.

*Sally darling, I've been to see the adjutant, requested a few days' leave but I must warn you though that things are getting very busy here, and it might not be possible – at least for some time. The day trips sound good.*

He couldn't bring himself to tell her about the ban on marriages, he'd have to do that in person.

*Please keep writing as much as you can. Every time I see your letters I feel so good – lost when the mailman has nothing from you.*

He continued with the language of love and ended with:

*I desire nothing more in life than to spend it with you.*
*All that I am is yours.*

*John*

# CHAPTER TWENTY-ONE

One day, on his way back to the mess for coffee, Walter Raus paused by the doors into the private chapel of the estate. He had no conscious idea of what it was that made him hesitate, then tentatively turn the large handle and push on the heavy oak door. Later, he wondered whether it had been because of their wedding.

Until that day he hadn't set foot in a church for . . . well many years, not since he had joined the Hitler Youth, in fact.

Although his parents had been quite regular churchgoers, and he was nominally a Lutheran, the Movement discouraged any form of membership of other organizations, secular as well as spiritual.

Frankly, his parents didn't seem to bother if he did not go to services on a Sunday; they were themselves, after the horrendous inflation and social unrest of the twenties and thirties, very much National Socialists. Somehow they managed, as did so many of their generation, to be both, but never seemed to worry about him; probably they were proud of his progress in the new order.

He eased open the heavy door. It gave a prolonged, enormous screech.

Inside it was cool, musty, and deeply quiet.

He walked slowly up the stone-floored aisle and stood before the carved altar. Beyond it was a round stained-glass window depicting Christ ascending to heaven.

It all looked very much older than he expected, medieval in fact. On impulse he sat down on an old chair in the front row.

It was as if, for a moment, the whole world, or his world of military discipline, of noise and brutal violence, had ceased to exist.

He didn't know how long he had been there – two minutes or ten, when the door gave out its screech and footsteps sounded on the stone floor.

He stood up – turned.

The little priest in his flowing black cassock edged with red piping pulled up with a start as the towering SS officer, dressed in his own black uniform, suddenly reared up before him.

For a second neither spoke, then Walter, aware of the startled, frightened look on the old abbé's face said gently in French:

'Good morning, father.'

The little priest seemed to recover. He nodded.

'Good morning to you.'

Walter, hands behind his back, swung his body from side to side for emphasis as he said: 'I have been admiring your church.'

The priest came nearer.

'Thank you. It is beautiful, is it not?'

Walter nodded. 'It is indeed. How old is it? It seems much earlier than the house?'

The priest explained.

'Yes, the original house was in fact a castle but was ransacked and burnt down in one of the wars and was rebuilt twice over the years, the last time in 1736. The church was left largely untouched except for a superficial make-over of the front to blend with the rest of the place.'

Walter, still with his hands clasped behind his back looked up at the vaulted, dark-beamed roof, then down to the walls. An effigy of a man in medieval chain mail, hands clasped in prayer, lay against one wall, a woman in long robes on the one opposite.

The priest said: 'This is the church of the family, and the estate.'

Walter nodded at the tomb. 'And he was?'

'Sir Guy de Lyons. He was killed on a crusade. They brought his body back in a cask of cognac.'

Walter grinned. He'd rather have drunk the cognac.

He knew they would never bring his body back in such a manner. In fact, he would be lucky to get a last resting place at all: he'd be blown to bits, probably.

He smiled at the priest.

'Crusader eh? You could say that about us. We are on a great crusade – to unite Europe and push back the Asian hordes.'

The little priest's face suddenly became immobile.

'This is a house of God. You should remove your hat.'

Walter looked at him, didn't say anything more, and didn't trust himself. But the man was brave, he gave him that. He walked down the aisle, opened the creaking door and stepped out into the sunlight.

What had he expected?

They belonged to two different ideologies.

Nonetheless, for a few minutes there, he had felt at peace with the world.

# CHAPTER TWENTY-TWO

In the evening Maddie took him to a favourite pub in Hampstead, an old coaching inn with a cobbled courtyard and dark timber frames.

They travelled on the underground, eventually emerging into the daylight of North London, after riding up in an elevator that she explained was the deepest shaft in the system.

The pub overlooked the Heath. It was early and still quiet.

They sat by a window, watching people enjoy the last of the sunlight. Kites were being flown, with tails, made from old newspaper.

The kites swooped and soared, and crashed to the ground. Several women were strolling along, pushing large black prams with spoked wheels and hoods.

Dogs ran after balls and a crowd of boys in short trousers and girls in dresses with puff sleeves and white ankle socks played tag.

It all looked so peaceful with the shadows lengthening as the sun set behind a row of poplar trees. The war might be a million miles away.

When they'd finished their drinks she said: 'Do you mind fish and chips again tonight? I don't know what else we can eat.'

'Of course not.'

They walked to a shop near the pub, queueing as a man and woman worked at a huge ornate and mirrored frying machine, the woman emptying a tub of freshly cut potatoes into the boiling lard with a great splash and hiss. A cloud of vapour rose up past the white wall tiles, which were inset with coloured scenes of fish, bubbles and seaweed.

When they were outside again, Maddie showed him what to do, ripping a hole in the newspaper wrapping and fishing out a steaming chip. 'It keeps them hot.'

He followed suit, his fingers closing around the crispy battered middle of the fish. He tore a piece off, brought it out, blowing gently on it as he realized how hot it was.

It tasted terrific.

They strolled on, stopping to watch as children, up a cul-de-sac where the front doors of the terraced houses opened straight out on to the pavement, played hopscotch on the slabs. Some girls were doing handstands against a wall, their dresses tucked into their dark navy knickers. Others were skipping, jumping in and out in turn as two others turned the rope, chanting as they did so:

The farmer wants a wife
The farmer wants a wife
Hi Ho Hi Ho
The farmer wants a wife
The wife wants a child
The wife wants a child . . .

Maddie chuckled. 'I used to sing that.'

Boys had chalked the outline of a wicket on a wooden double gate leading into a work-yard, and were using a cricket bat to swipe a bald tennis ball all over the place. It flew his way; he caught it with one hand, throwing it back.

He nodded. 'They seem OK.'

She frowned. 'Children are resilient. Since the big evacuations of the early days a lot have come back now as you can see. I don't know if that is wise.'

She'd sensed, as a lot of Londoners had, that the so-called 'nuisance' raids were increasing in frequency.

When she had finished she balled up her newsprint, put it into a bin and put her arm through his.

'What would you like to do for the rest of the evening?'

He hesitated. 'Well. . . .'

Maddie, thinking he was being reticent about something encouraged him with: 'Go on?'

Robbie was sheepish. 'I'd like nothing better than another quiet night in.' He added hurriedly. 'If that's all right with you?'

Her eyes flashed with warmth. She squeezed his arm, murmured: 'Me too. Come on.'

Relieved, he chuckled, but it made him think. What would his mother make of him, living like a married man with a girl who was happy to be his 'wife'?

He shook his head; thought the war was eroding all their morals as young people lived for the moment.

And he was no different.

Maddie pulled the blackout curtain as he waited by the light switch. He flicked it on as soon as the place was plunged into pitch blackness.

She nodded. 'Take your shoes off. Switch on the wireless.'

In his socks he went to the brown wooden radio set, shaped like a pointed arch with a fretwork pattern on the front of the speaker, and turned a knob. A light came on behind the programme panel, and the set started to buzz. He twiddled the tuner as the indicator line passed Hilversum and Luxembourg. The sound changed to a succession of weird whistles, rising and falling accompanied by bursts of static. He guessed it was either the fault of the valves or of the Germans jamming the radio waves.

Eventually, the wireless emitted the syrupy tones of many saxophones. They kissed and caressed all the way through 'Why Do Robins Sing in December?', ending up on the sofa, he lying stretched out with his head on her lap as she slowly played a hand through his hair.

Eventually the announcer's cut-glass voice came out of the set:

*And so we say goodnight from Rainbow Corner here in London, and the band of the AEF under their conductor Major Glenn Miller, United States Army Air Force. Goodnight.*

There was a silence as Maddie stared dreamily into the yellowy-red bars of the gas fire, and then the chimes of Big Ben rang out. When the last note died away the announcer said gravely: '*This is the BBC Home Service. Here is the news and this is Alvar Lidell reading it. Today, Soviet Forces under . . .*'

She pushed Robbie's head gently up, reached for the wireless and turned it off.

'Let's forget the war.' She went to the table, refilled their whisky glasses. 'I want to play – just for you. Stay here.'

She went into the bedroom. He heard the piano lid go up and the shuffling of music sheets.

She began with *Clair de Lune*, then a Chopin étude that evoked a timeless feeling of peace.

When she finished he swung his legs to the floor, picked up the half-empty bottle and went into the bedroom.

Her glass was on a cork mat on the top of the piano. He went to replenish it, but she waved him away. After he had filled his own glass he set the bottle down on the cabinet and stretched out on the bed.

'Maddie?'

Shuffling her music she looked over her shoulder, answered expectantly. 'Yes?'

'Would you play for me – naked?'

Shocked, she stared at him. He knew how much her music meant to her, so why. . . ?

All the distrust and fear of men rushed back. Had she made a mistake? Was he like her father – were they all the same?

'I don't understand.'

Unaware of the turmoil raging inside her, Robbie said simply:

'You are beautiful and I want to be the only one in the world to see you perform like that – our secret, because I love you so much.' Time seemed to stand still, and then she slowly stood up, still staring at him. Her eyes never left his as she undressed.

Totally naked she answered:

'And I love you.'

She went back to the piano. From where he was he could see sheet music already open on the rest, covered in great clumps of notes that looked like mountain ranges, then her naked slim body blocked the view, dimples appearing on her bottom as she sat down. She began to play.

The piano exploded with great chords of Rachmaninov's music, vibrating as she traversed the keyboard. Her whole body lifted from the stool to add strength to her exertions. It amazed him that such power could come from such a slender figure.

He listened transfixed, as the room resonated with brilliant sound, a musical experience that overwhelmed him in its passionate intensity. He may have had no conception of the hours and hours of practice she had put in, the nights going over and over certain passages, the tears, the rages, the pain in her fingers, but he was suddenly aware of her prodigious talent.

When she finished, and the last chord slowly died away there was absolute silence.

After some moments she turned, her pink nipples rising and falling as she caught her breath.

After a pause he said, 'You will marry me won't you Maddie?'

Seconds passed.

'Yes.'

That night they slept wrapped in each other's arms, undisturbed by a distant raid on the East End, the noise only making them stir once, when the sharp crack of a stray bomb falling in nearby Tottenham Court Road brought down a fine dust in the kitchen and rattled the sash window in the sitting room.

# CHAPTER TWENTY-THREE

A month passed before John and Sally met again. She, in her navy-blue uniform, hair pulled tightly up under her blue Wren hat stepped down from the carriage on to Swindon station, looking anxiously around for him. Her steel helmet and gas mask were slung from one shoulder, she carried a brown weekend case in her other hand. There was no sign of John. The platform was packed with soldiers and civilians milling about, accompanied by the crash of boots and the whistles of the station staff organizing the departure of trains.

With an answering blast on the whistle her engine vented a great surge of steam over the rails in front of it, and began to move.

It was half a minute before the hissing guard's van went past and the track was empty.

'Sally.'

She heard him calling, couldn't see him anywhere until he called out again.

'Sally, over here.'

She saw him then, standing on the platform opposite, across the tracks.

He threw his arms wide. 'Sorry, got the wrong platform, then when the train came in there was such a crush I couldn't get over – but you've got to come this way to get out.'

Sally's heart had leapt on seeing him. She waved. 'Stay there, I'm coming.'

John Fairfax watched as the slim figure, looking even slimmer in her uniform, picked up her case and walked swiftly to the steps of the bridge. She looked so different with her hair pinned up – beautiful in yet another way. He couldn't wait for her to reach him, took the stairs two at a time. They met on the bridge. She dropped her case as he picked her up and swung her round, holding her tightly to him. With her free hand she held on to her hat.

When he set her down they kissed – long and tenderly as a group of GI's passed by, wolf-whistling. He was oblivious to it all.

When at last he released her she was breathless but happy. He picked up her case.

'Come on – we've a bus to catch.'

Outside the station they just caught one as it started pulling away. John pushed her up on to the platform before he swung himself on with her case. They slumped into the bench seat just inside the doorway. The female clippie started her round of the bus.

'Where to, luv?'

He told her. She pulled out two cardboard tickets and punched them with her machine. Paid, she carried on down the aisle, bumping from seat to seat as the vehicle jerked through its gears.

'Where are we going?'

He squeezed her hand.

'I've found an inn by a river just outside of town.'

In the little reception area they had to sign in.

Sally kept her gloves on as he wrote Lieutenant and Mrs J Fairfax.

The old man watched, turned the book his way, then reached behind him to find the key to their room.

'There we are, sir.'

He said nothing further, even though Sally's cheeks seemed to be burning off her face.

'You'll find your room at the top of the stairs, first on the left.'

'Thank you.'

John picked up Sally's case and stood back to let her go first up the steep, tightly turning staircase.

At the top she stopped outside the door and waited while he inserted the key and turned the lock. He pushed the door open, then, without warning, picked her up and carried her in, flicking the door shut behind them with his foot.

Sally gasped, then chuckled.

'Is this because I just became Mrs Fairfax?'

'Yep.'

It had been on his mind all day, since he had found out that the ban on marrying could not be applied to non-enlisted officers. Thank God he hadn't said anything.

They stood there, looking around at the room, decorated with faded wallpaper with hundreds of Monarchs of the Glen going up the walls.

She giggled. 'Stags, how very appropriate.'

That afternoon they went to a tea dance. When they got there couples were moving around the dance floor. They joined in, managing only one circuit before the orchestra conductor, holding a violin, called, 'Next dance, please.'

She held on to John's arm as they joined the throng leaving the floor.

They did dance some more, but a Paul Jones was announced, where the girls formed a circle holding hands facing outwards, and the men did the same facing them, until the music abruptly stopped and then you danced with the person facing you. John and Sally decided they'd had enough.

That evening they decided to go to the pictures. He told her she had a choice between *For Whom the Bell Tolls;* with Gary Cooper and Ingrid Bergman, or *Heaven Can Wait* with Gene Tierney and Don Ameche. She chose *For Whom The Bell Tolls,* a story of love and duty in the Spanish Civil War. Ingrid Bergman was a favourite of hers.

They sat through a supporting Western with Hopalong Cassidy, before the lights went up for the interval.

When the lights dimmed once more a spotlight cut the darkness, falling on a man in a white dinner-jacket riding up out of the floor on a Wurlitzer organ.

For ten minutes the audience sang along with the tunes, ending with 'Mairzy doats' and 'Don't sit under the apple tree with anyone else but me'.

The organ started to descend, the organist playing himself out with 'Underneath the spreading chestnut tree'.

He was still playing when the spotlight suddenly pinched out.

The second half of the evening began with the British Pathé News, heralded by its crowing cock. Items on the war effort, including the sideways launch of a liberty ship, were followed by footage of the arrival of Bob Hope and Bing Crosby to entertain the troops in England.

At last the big movie started.

Later, when they all filed out into the darkness she put her arm through his, and said: 'It's a nice night, let's walk back.'

They stopped once, sat on a bench and lit up. It was a clear night, with millions of stars twinkling in the velvet blackness above them, the same stars that were looking down at the awesome struggle going on in the East, and the growing strength of the Allied Army all around.

An army to which he belonged.

An army that soon would be committed to battle.

# CHAPTER TWENTY-FOUR

Inge had come out of the shelter into an unimaginable scene from hell.

Everything round about seemed on fire, and the streets were littered with hundreds of corpses – men, women – some holding children, old people, naked people, clothed people, charred people – *dead people.*

Some had lost arms and legs.

Some looked peaceful.

Some were contorted with the pain of a terrible end.

Others were without faces, burnt away by lumps of phosphorous.

Quickly the civil defence organized themselves into parties to collect the dead and stack them in piles three and four deep.

It was women who were doing the work; those men who were left were too old or disabled, apart from some members of the Hitler Youth.

She struggled with three others with the corpse of a woman whose body had become fused with that of a child, naked except for her little socks, pressed to her mother's bosom.

She wondered what these women toiling around her on their gruesome task were thinking.

The other day one of the nurses had stood in the middle of the ward and screamed out. 'There is no gas, no electricity, no water. The telephones don't work. There is nothing to eat.'

She had looked wildly around her. 'Any party worker better keep out of my way.'

It was astounding, since she was a leading National Socialist herself, who gave lessons in race theory to the young new recruits in the nursing school.

She had been hustled away. Later it was said she'd had a nervous breakdown and was on the sick list.

Morale was plummeting, especially amongst women, with the

incessant bombing and the rising casualty list amongst men serving in the armed forces.

Publically, there had been a marked decline in the trust of the people for those around the Führer, who were accused of not taking their share in the nation's sacrifice, of feathering their own nests whether it was with food or the construction of deep air-raid shelters for themselves and their families, and continuing to have their sons sent to safe postings away from the Eastern front.

Inge felt guilty that, thank God, Walter was in France; but then, he'd done his bit for the Fatherland against the Russians.

She got on with her gruesome work, aware that there was less than an hour to go before the start of her shift.

If she got the time she would dash off a quick letter, reassuring him that she was all right. She also wondered whether it was too premature to tell him, that they were expecting their firstborn. Then, as they heaved the body of the woman and child on to the pile, she paused to look down on the pitiful remains. It made up her mind.

That night, by the light of an oil lamp glowing in the deep cellar beneath the hospital, surrounded by patients on trolleys jammed side by side, with the distant crump of bombs that brought down little spirals of dust, she began:

*My beloved husband*
*I love you, and you love me, so you have a right to know the truth as soon as possible, especially in these uncertain times. Although it is very early to be saying this, I believe we are to be blessed with a baby some time early in the New Year; a year I sincerely hope will bring peace to our beloved Fatherland. I hope this news will give you great happiness – as it has me.*

*I am very tired tonight my darling, so I beg your forgiveness for this being only a short note.*

*Tomorrow evening, when I am rested, I promise to write again, and give you all the other news.*

*So, goodnight my husband, sweet dreams. Keep yourself safe for me and for young Kurt or Anna.*

*Your loving wife, Inge*

# CHAPTER TWENTY-FIVE

Robbie had been at a bleak windswept airfield in the north, mastering the rugged difficult Typhoon, a single seat fighter-bomber of enormous power.

Now he had been posted to an operational squadron. He sat down in the mess and put pen to paper.

*Dear Maddie*
*A very quick note. Have just finished the course, and they are sending me down south, in a bit of a rush – so we should see a lot more of each other from now on.*

*Have you been to see your local priest yet? I will do whatever is necessary to marry you – as quickly as possible please.*

*I'll write again as soon as I'm settled in.*

*Rushing to catch the post. Can't wait to leave this god-forsaken place.*

*With all my love,*

*Robbie x x x*

He followed it with the usual crosses – to hell with the censor laughing at him.

Maddie entered the tube station, got a ticket and stepped on the escalator. Down on the platform the warm rush of warm air pushed out of the tunnel by the arriving train was, on this cold blustery day in early May, welcome.

Pressing hard against the jam-packed Londoners, the doors closed with a hiss of air pressure. Electric motors whining, the train clattered down the length of the platform, where wooden bunks still remained in place for use as a night-time shelter. Then it plunged into the tunnel, where the pipes on the dark walls rose and fell outside the windows as they rocked and lurched and the lights flickered.

Maddie had spent all afternoon studying with a Jewish lady, Madam Kaplinsky, at the latter's home. She was a refugee from Berlin where she had been a teacher at the conservatoire. But on Krystallnacht in 1939 she had decided that enough was enough, and there was no future in a Germany under Hitler, not even perhaps, life itself. Considering how late she had left it, she had been lucky to get out, but despite all that had happened to her and her family she was also a great champion of German music.

'It represents the finest outpouring of a civilization which has been seduced by the forces of darkness, my dear,' she said with a pronounced accent.

At a Lyons shop Maddie managed to consume a cup of tea and a Chelsea bun before she went on to one of her hotels. It seemed strange, but she kept thinking that he would appear out of the crowd.

But he didn't.

By the time she had finished and begun her walk home the wind had abated. She passed a group of GIs who wolf-whistled and called after her, but otherwise there seemed remarkably few people about.

When she got home Maddie felt very tired, it had been a long day, but her heart lifted when she saw his letter on the mat.

She snatched it up and sat on the stairs as she devoured every word.

Yes, he had been to see his RC Padre and they'd had a long chat. The padre had given him some leaflets and a small book. Maddie lowered his letter.

But it upset her. Why should he have to do anything?

For the first time in her life she began to think the unthinkable, that she might not care what the church thought.

After all, she had already broken the rules with Robbie.

Later, changed for bed, with her dressing-gown wrapped tightly about her, and with a cup of Ovaltine, she tucked her legs up under her on the sofa, and began to write to him. The radio was down low, the soft dance music making her feel very sad and lonely, especially when a woman started singing 'Somewhere over the rainbow'.

She stopped writing, and wondered where their rainbow would end.

Robbie was shown the tent he was to share with three others. The airfield was a totally under-canvas affair, occupied by two squadrons dispersed on three sides of the temporary runways made of Somerfelt tracking.

The service wing was set in a nearby field, the larger marquees that served as messes and kitchens in another. Only the headquarters was under a solid roof – of sorts – in an old barn.

Less than a mile away was another airstrip; the congestion in the South of England was now nearing the limit, with army camps and airfields cheek by jowl.

For the first time Robbie got a sense of the awe-inspiring build-up for the coming invasion.

After a restless night on his camp bed, with a squadron leader next to him who snored like a foghorn, Robbie sat down in the mess tent to a plate of real eggs and bacon.

The place was busy, with a constant coming and going of pilots and the babble of voices.

Suddenly a flight lieutenant came in through the open canvas door, blew a hunting horn, then shouted:

'Briefing in the ops room – ten minutes. We've got a show.'

Men stuffed in mouthfuls of food, some put their egg and bacon between slices of bread and grabbed mugs of tea, taking them with them as they made a bolt for the door.

Within half an hour they were blasting out over the sea at 200 feet, keeping well below the enemy radar.

The dark streak of the French coast appeared, and when they were ten miles out the wing leader took them up to 3,000 feet.

Caught unawares, the 88mm radar-predicted flak batteries only managed a light reaction, then they were past and going up to 5,000 feet.

Minutes went by. He constantly scoured the broken cloud above for any sign of enemy 190s or 109s.

He was aware of the powerful shapes of the Typhoons fanning out all around him, gently rising and falling in the turbulent air.

The wing leader suddenly broke the R/T silence.

'Target: large train, eleven o'clock. Open out – we'll give it one pass.'

When it was his turn Robbie put the aircraft into a shallow dive. He found the train in the gunsight, the first two carriages were already on fire.

When the engine filled the entire sight he pressed the tit, and watched his 20mm cannon hit the boiler, which blew up in a great eruption of steam.

Minutes later the wing leader was pulling the formation round in a climbing turn on to another freight train, this time with a flak wagon attached that was already pumping up shells at them.

'Blue 2, take the wagon. Blue 3, the engine.'

Robbie rolled over, dived down. The red tracer seemed to be coming right at him. Sweating, he held his nerve. At 700 yards out he opened fire, walking the burst right into the flak wagon.

As he flashed over at 200 feet he was aware of an explosion that rocked the aircraft so much he feared the wings would tear off.

All day they kept up the pressure, doing two, sometimes three sorties a day.

And the next day.

And the next.

Attacking airfields was the most dangerous. They were heavily protected with anti-aircraft guns that put up curtains of automatic fire through which they had to fly.

They began to lose aircraft: some exploded in the air, others dived straight into the ground as the deadly flak found its mark.

Great columns of oily black smoke rose into the air, marking the spot where a man they had shared breakfast with had just vanished from the face of the earth.

Rarely was it the Luftwaffe that engaged them in combat – so many fighters had to be deployed over the Reich against the Allies non-stop strategic bombing onslaught.

At the end of the final week, late in the evening as the sun was setting, they moved smoothly out of formation and banked, stream-landing on the undulating strip, taxiing in, throwing up clouds of dust and dried grass. They had achieved the virtual paralysis of the enemy railway system in northern France, and ruled the roads with a rod of iron. In daylight no German convoy could move with impunity on the long straight roads without attracting the attention of the marauding Typhoons. The AOC 11 group sent a signal of congratulation.

But Robbie was already aware of the attrition rate, of replacements arriving, looking very young and bewildered, uncertain and frightened. It was no wonder that some of them scrambled with propellers in course pitch, or burnt out their brakes. Some got themselves killed without ever meeting the enemy, like the boy who had only left school six months before. He didn't envy the CO writing to the grieving parents.

He began to wonder how long he would last, especially when the Allies were fighting on the mainland. The rate of losses could only increase.

Robbie was hoping he might eventually get a 'forty-eight'; he needed so desperately to see Maddie. Then word came through that they were to stand down for twenty-four hours to obtain maximum serviceability, and that all aircraft were to be painted with black and white stripes on the rear fuselage and both wings top and bottom. They all knew that they were the invasion identity markings. No one was to leave the camp, or send a letter, or telephone.

They were sealed off from the outside world.

As somebody in the mess laconically remarked as he sipped his beer, and smoked a cigarette, blowing out smoke towards the ceiling: 'Looks like the balloon is about to go up.'

It was 3 June, 1944.

# CHAPTER TWENTY-SIX

John Fairfax was drinking a cup of coffee in a small anteroom of the Officers Club. Most others were reading newspapers from home. He had a notepad on his knees, and was writing to Sally. The wireless beside him was on. A show was just being announced, called ITMA. The British had a weird sense of humour. Someone called Tommy Handley entertained a succession of strange characters with funny voices, who came and went with the sound of a door opening and closing. They each seemed to have famous opening lines, because the audience screamed with laughter, especially at a Mrs Mopp, an office char, whatever that was, and her 'Can I do you now Sir?'

It was followed by the news. He noticed that others lowered their papers as they listened to the reports on the fierce fighting at Monte Cassino in Italy. The Germans were entrenched in the now ruined monastery, blasted by heavy Allied bombing, and still resisting.

There could be no doubt about the fighting qualities of the enemy.

It didn't bode well.

Sally found she had been posted to the joint communication and planning centre at Norfolk House in London.

As she was being interviewed by a brigadier her gaze ran around his office.

On the walls were great boards covered in postcards of beaches. She recognized one of them.

'That's Normandy, isn't it, sir?'

She pointed to one postcard that showed a large sandy beach.

Immediately the brigadier, who had been perusing her documents with especial reference to her security clearances, looked up sharply.

His moustache quivered. 'You know the area well?'

Sally nodded.

'Oh yes, sir. A crowd of us went there for a whole summer, cycling along that coast and taking the boat back from Cherbourg.'

The light glinted on the brigadier's monocle.

'Have you any snaps?'

She winced. 'Yes, lots, but only of us silly girls sitting on beaches and walls and the like, and in the surrounding countryside eating cheese and drinking cheap wine, and generally making fools of ourselves. Mind you, for two weeks we did help out selling crêpes for a man on the beach.'

She coloured under his continuing stare.

'I was very young, sir.'

But all he did was suddenly to stand up and say: 'Come with me. I'd like you to meet some chaps who will be very interested to hear your comments. And where are you billeted – is that where the photos are?'

Confused, she too stood up as well as he came round the desk.

'No, sir, they're at my parents' house.'

'Where's that?'

'They live in Olney now, sir – in Buckinghamshire.'

'Are they on the telephone?'

'Yes, sir.'

'Then ring them – use mine. Get them to dig them out immediately. I'll arrange for an RAF guard to pick them up and have them flown down to Northolt today.'

Eyes wide with amazement, Sally was ushered to his phone. He got an outside line, then handed her the receiver.

Even as she spoke to her father she knew now where the invasion was going to land, where John would be in great danger.

Her heart sank as she remembered the 'bocage' – the densely hedged little lanes and tiny fields of Normandy. In places it was not unlike the lanes of Cornwall.

John received only one letter from Sally before the sequestration started. She was looking forward to their lives together. She loved him dearly; they were a good team weren't they? Please, please, be careful.

He frowned, disappointed that they had not yet been able to marry. Still, he had taken his courage in both hands and had written to Betty at her home address, to be forwarded to wherever she was now.

In the letter he had put it as bluntly as he could, that he'd changed, and that, as a couple, their relationship was a thing of the past. He did not mention that he'd met someone else but guessed she would suspect that; women knew. It was one of the hardest things he'd ever done, and he realized for the first time just how much he had cared for her.

But it was not like the way he felt about Sally.

That evening the orders that everyone had been expecting were posted.

All over southern England, units, British, American and Canadian were being sealed off from the outside world, with the warning that anyone caught outside the camp would be court-martialled. For the first time the detailed planning of 'Overlord': the intended breaching of Hitler's Atlantic Wall, and the invasion of Western Europe, was revealed. Second Lieutenant John Fairfax found that they, the 101st Airborne Division, were to be dropped near Carentan on the flank of the seaborne forces landing at Utah Beach.

That night he wrote to Sally from his tent as, outside, troops wearing German uniforms and carrying German weapons wandered around, the butt of wisecracks, but with the serious intention of familiarizing the troopers with what their enemy looked like in real life.

He knew she would not get the letter for at least a few days, maybe a week or two. But it had to be written in case. . . . He didn't let his mind dwell on that.

The next day, the fourth of June, they were issued with all their ammunition, ten dollars' worth of francs and an escape kit containing a silk map with a tiny brass compass.

They had a practice session of the verbal challenges and replies to be used, the challenge 'Flash', the reply 'Thunder' and the response 'Welcome'. Small, cheap metal crickets were issued, one squeeze – *click-clack* – to be answered by two squeezes.

These challenges were important, because some confusion could be expected during the course of a jump made by night.

By now they were all on edge, chain-smoking, and rechecking their equipment. Some of the fellows shaved their heads, or got Mohawk cuts, leaving a strip of short hair running from forehead to the back of the head.

Their last meal was steak, with peas and mashed potatoes, followed by ice cream, the first they had tasted since they had arrived in England.

Everybody guessed that it meant they were on for that night.

The food seemed to form a hard undigested lump in John's stomach.

Major General Maxwell Taylor came round the regiments. He stopped in front of John Fairfax. 'Where you from, son?'

He told him. The general slapped him on the shoulder.

'Get you back there as soon as we can,' he said, and moved on.

They began to get ready, smearing their faces with dark camouflage cream. But as the evening progressed they looked at each other, worried by the increasingly gusty wind.

The message eventually came through to stand down. Eisenhower had postponed because of the weather.

It was a strange feeling, a mixture of disappointment and profound relief.

He joined the men watching a movie with Cary Grant called *Mr Lucky*. They all hoped the name would prove prophetic.

He had a restless night, couldn't sleep, kept getting out his flashlight and looking at her photo.

Next day the gale had quietened; the blustery wind lessened as the day wore on, and the sky cleared to broken cloud.

At lunchtime on the fifth of June, the word came down that it was on for that night, Eisenhower was taking a gamble on a predicted gap in the weather.

It was a long job kitting up for the jump, but when he'd got to his webbing belt and braces, his .45 pistol, water canteen, shovel, first-aid kit, and had strapped his gas mask to his left leg and his bayonet to his right one, he was ready at last.

He climbed with his men into the waiting trucks, their parachutes and leg bags were thrown in after them.

They were driven to the waiting planes, which stood in rows, one behind the other, receding into the distance.

It was quite a heartening sight.

Beside their C47, with its white invasion stripes on its wings and fuselage, they helped each other into the harness and main parachute in its backpack, with the reserve hooked on their front. Over everything went the Mae West life jacket.

Some of the men had found cans of black and green paint, and some charcoal, and had daubed their faces like Indian braves.

There was nothing to do now but sit under the aircraft wings and wait.

Every now and then men struggled to their feet, went to the edge of the runway, relieved themselves, and then sat down again. A few minutes later they did it all over again.

He knew what it was: *nerves*.

He did it himself, several times.

Every passing hour it got worse. Some men openly prayed, others thumbed creased paperbacks, or just stared down between their legs, lost in thought.

He kept his mind on Sally, wondered what she was doing at that moment. He checked his watch; probably she'd be tucked up in bed. He wished he was there beside her, feeling her soft warmth, smelling her hair.

He was still thinking of her when whistles blew and the call to mount up rang out.

John Fairfax pushed the men into their plane; some were carrying as much as 150 pounds, and were unable to climb the short flight of steps unaided.

Engines started, the roar making it difficult for them to hear each other.

They'd been given a pack of papers earlier, back in the hangars. There was a message from Eisenhower. Sitting at last in his seat, before the doors were closed, John read it again.

*Soldiers, sailors and airmen of the Allied Expeditionary Force. You are about to embark upon the great crusade toward which we have striven these many months. The eyes of the world are upon you. . . .*

It ended with:

*Good luck! And let us all beseech the blessings of Almighty God upon this great and noble undertaking.*

The door was shut and they rumbled and bounced and vibrated for what seemed like for ever. Then at last, they were roaring down the runway. The vibration ceased as the C47 clawed its way into the night sky.

They were on their way to war.

# CHAPTER TWENTY-SEVEN

Walter Raus had enjoyed a good dinner; the mess unterscharführer did a wonderful job from local ingredients. Normally he would take his glass of cognac outside, light one of his precious and dwindling supply of cigars, and contemplate the beautiful countryside from the terrace.

But tonight the wind was still gusting, and there had been bursts of rain all day.

So Walter found a comfortable leather easy chair, and a book from the château's library. He spoke and read French fluently.

Later, he was invited to join a card game with the brigadeführer and two oberführers.

The atmosphere was relaxed.

In view of the weather there would obviously be no invasion. Even now Field Marshal Erin Rommel was back in Germany seeing his family on leave; it was his wife's fiftieth birthday and word had it that he had stopped off in Paris to buy her some shoes.

But to those in the know the real intention of his visit was to petition Hitler, personally, for more anti-aircraft guns, and immediate control of the panzer forces.

They played until quite late, and were even entertained at about midnight by reports of an exchange between a corps headquarters in St Lô and a Luftwaffe company on the island of Guernsey who were operating a radar station, and who insisted that enemy aircraft, some towing gliders, were approaching. Their regimental commander had demanded that an air alert should be called.

Apparently a sarcastic general staff officer had rung back with the message that: *'The Gentlemen of the Staff wish their comrades on the island a good night; and we advise you to be on the lookout for small ghosts only, and urge caution before you sow any more wild oats.'*

They had all laughed and called for another round of cognac.

When Walter Raus eventually went to bed, winding up his wristwatch as was his habit and placing it on to his bedside cabinet, he stretched out his hand to turn off the light – and caught sight of his silver-framed photograph of Inge.

He was not given to demonstrative gestures, but for some reason – possibly the amount of cognac he had imbibed – he picked it up and stared at it for some time.

He still could not believe his luck that Inge loved him; she could have had so many more handsome and desirable men.

He gently brushed his lips to hers. Feeling stupid he replaced it and snapped off the light.

In the dark he listened as the wind rattled the old window.

# CHAPTER TWENTY-EIGHT

Maddie presented herself for the last tutorial of the day, with Robbie's latest letter tucked into her pocket. She was feeling upset, a bit emotional, as she knew now that he was back in the front line of the air offensive – back in danger again.

The tall elegant figure of Sir Miles, dressed in a black jacket, from which a silk breast-pocket handkerchief draped down out of the top pocket, and pinstripe trousers, drawled sarcastically: 'Now then, Madeleine, you really do need to get down to some seriously hard work this term.'

Frankly, he had always found her to be technically competent, but lacking in colour, in emotion. But she would make a good teacher or accompanist.

'Let's start with this piece.'

He put some music on to the piano's music-rest.

She nodded, flexing her fingers, adjusting the stool to just the right height, and cleared all thoughts from her mind – except Robbie. He would always be there, as long as she lived.

She drove her fingers down on to the keys, and the first notes of Liszt's second Hungarian Rhapsody rang out. Frowning, halfway through the piece Sir Miles looked up from the score he was following. Surely there was a new depth to her playing that had been absent before – more – soul? Had he misjudged her?

The girl was good, very good indeed. In fact, as he turned a page, and briefly looked up at her again, saw a lock of hair falling across her forehead as she bent over the piano, and her fingers dancing on the keyboard, he would say – quite exceptional.

It was as if she was a different girl – no, a woman with a new-found maturity.

*

When Maddie eventually got home she put the kettle on, went into the bedroom and changed for bed. She felt very tired; she was aware that she had missed her monthly period for the second time, knew that she would very soon have to see Doctor Pedlow, her kind old Irish GP.

She took her cup of Ovaltine into the bedroom, intent on sitting up in bed and writing to Robbie; then she decided that perhaps she should wait a day or so – until she had been to the doctor and had had her pregnancy confirmed.

Instead she thought of playing something that suited her mood. She had a stack of music from the shows and films, from which she often added to her repertoire at the hotels. Shuffling through them she came upon the 'Warsaw Concerto' from the 1940 film *Dangerous Moonlight*, a popular story of a pianist playing on as Warsaw crashed and burned all around him.

On impulse she put it up on the music-rest, and began to pick out the notes, tentatively at first, then with increasing vigour.

As she did so, ships of the greatest invasion fleet the world had ever known were leaving harbour, and grinding through still rough seas towards the coast of Normandy.

They were all packed into the operations tent at midnight, Robbie cross-legged on the floor just at the feet of the briefing party, as Eisenhower's exhortation to the great crusade was read out. The ships were already at sea.

'Overlord' was destined for the beaches of Normandy. There was a ripple of voices at the announcement. It was a long way across and the wind was still gusting strongly, but the met officer had come on and told them the weather was expected to improve, at least for enough time to get the army ashore; it would be risky, but Eisenhower had weighed up the options. The next favourable tide for a landing would be some weeks later, and the increasing problems of morale and secrecy were too great to contemplate any further delay.

They were tasked to patrol to the west of the beachhead in an air protection role: nothing was to get through. They were given careful instructions, as vast transport fleets carrying airborne forces would be operating cross-channel.

John Fairfax sat in the dark, the fear like a cold dead thing in the pit of his stomach. Only the red glow from cigarettes showed the lines of sitting men.

A lot of the troopers had gulped airsickness pills as soon as the engines had started up, and were now so drowsy that they were barely awake. But John was, his head filled with thoughts of Sally and when they would meet again.

As they skirted the islands of Jersey and Guernsey, anti-aircraft fire sent tracers into the sky, too far away to reach them, but it was worrying – would the batteries on the mainland hear and see them?

The pilot called back.

'Five minutes.'

The crew chief removed the door of the plane, blasting them with fresh air. John Fairfax leaned out slightly, could see the dark outline of the coast going by underneath.

'Get ready,' he yelled.

At that moment German 88mm guns opened up. The exploding shells hurt their ears, bounced the aircraft up and down as if they were in a violent storm.

Searing light flashed, then they were plunged into darkness, but not before he'd seen the densely packed C47s in tight formation all around.

Tracer started coming up, sweeping the sky, rattling against the fuselage like a shower of pebbles. Somebody yelled: 'I've been hit.'

Another jolting crack and the plane lifted as if it had struck the ground.

Framed in his doorway there was the sickening sight of the C47 on their wing exploding in a ball of yellow flame, plunging to earth like a flaming meteor, taking the remains of men they had known and trained with for the last year. The trooper next to him suddenly heaved his guts up, splashing their contents all over the floor.

Cries could be heard in the darkness.

'Jesus, let us outta here.'

'Let's go.'

The plane began to speed up as it went into a shallow dive. The red light came on, dimly showing their tightly drawn faces half-lost in the shadows of their helmets.

'Stand up!' he shouted.

Troopers struggled to their feet, slipping on the vomit-covered floor as the aircraft bucked and rolled with the bombardment.

He ordered: 'Hook up.'

The troopers attached themselves to the anchor line.

John Fairfax hung on grimly, his mouth dry with fear. The moment was near when they would at last join battle with the enemy, that which he and millions of young Americans had been training for since they had answered their country's call.

Slipping and slithering on the greasy floor the troopers pushed forward, their bodies jammed hard against each other as they sought to stay on their feet and the plane swung violently from side to side.

More tracer came up. He could see that they were much lower than they should be, and there was a danger that the chutes wouldn't open in time. The tracer was now so thick it looked as if you could walk on it.

The green light suddenly glowed in the fuselage, the crew chief was screaming:

'Go, go, go.'

John Fairfax, whose hands were already on the outside of the door frame, leapt out into the void. The propeller blast ripped at him in the second before the static line pulled the back cover off his main chute, the canopy came out of the pack and, with a terrific crack, his harness wrenched his shoulders up to his ears. He swung wildly around like a rag doll. The plane had been going much too fast.

For a second the silence was deafening, and then it all exploded back again.

Below there were muzzle flashes and explosions, and all the tracer in the sky seemed to be coming up at him.

Between his legs he could see a house on fire, and figures moving about. Were they Germans about to shoot him as he hung helplessly in the sky? He tried to steer away.

Tracer bullets hit his canopy, leaving glowing holes. Less than a minute from jumping out of the plane he crashed into a hedgerow and fell through its thorny branches, ending up in a ditch. A French ditch.

Battered and shaken he released himself from his harness, then crawled to the top of one side of the ditch and looked around.

He could hear firefights going on for miles around: staccato bursts of automatic fire. Somewhere a church bell was ringing.

Overhead planes were roaring past, wave on wave, getting lower. Some were on fire, passing like fiery rockets in the night sky.

Weirdly he heard sounds like pumpkins smashing on to the ground;

it brought back memories of throwing them out of his dorm windows at Harvard during a rag.

Suddenly the last aircraft passed overhead, dangerously low, and was gone. The air armada had finished.

It all went quiet, even the rattle and pop-popping of far-off small arms died away. He seemed to be all alone in the world.

He tried a click-clack, but there was no answering call. Where was everybody?

Cautiously he got to his feet and, crouching, started to limp along the lane, heading towards where he thought the rendezvous point was. It was already clear to him that the regiment, and probably the whole division had been scattered over a wide area. It was chaos.

He tripped over something, and crashed painfully on to a tarred road. He'd made such a clatter that he lay there, Garand rifle at the ready, his finger tense on the trigger, his heart pounding, but nothing happened.

He rolled on to his side, and found himself in a warm sticky substance. He struggled to get out his flashlight with a hand made slippery with the greasiness of the substance.

When he switched it on the pool of light showed a black liquid. Oil?

He started to breathe a sigh of relief, and then the rest came into sight. His stomach spasmed, and hot bile spewed from his gagging mouth.

The man's head was split wide open, one eye facing to the night sky whence he had come, the other looking at his own teeth scattered on the road in front of him. As the light travelled down the body, it illuminated the trooper's guts, black and glistening coils spread all across the road. His half-opened parachute lay to one side.

John Fairfax knew then what the sound of pumpkins smashing to earth was. The planes had been less than 500 feet and going much too fast as the pilots panicked.

Shivering, he crawled away, still trying to vomit, and curled up in the ditch. It was just a boy lying out there, no more than eighteen or nineteen years old, killed before he had fired a shot for his country.

So much for the great crusade.

# CHAPTER TWENTY-NINE

'Sir . . . sir. . . .'

Walter came to with a start as the Gefreiter shook his shoulder. He shot bolt upright.

'What is it?'

'The Brigadeführer would like all officers downstairs – urgently.'

'Why – what's happened?'

The young Gefreiter looked excited.

'Lot of reports coming in, sir – of parachutists.'

Walter dressed hurriedly and went down to the operations room. The place was in turmoil. Telephones were incessantly ringing, and dispatch riders were coming and going.

Before a large table map of the northern French coast were groups of anxious-looking brother officers; others were arriving hurriedly all the time, some still pulling on their tunics.

The Brigadeführer turned to him.

'The reports of the landings are very widespread – more than just a localized raid.'

Walter frowned.

'But the weather, surely it can't be anything more than that, sir?'

The Brigadeführer clicked his teeth, half-turned.

'I agree, nevertheless I've informed army headquarters of the situation, and advised them that all our panzer units are ready for deployment with immediate effect. That decision, of course, rests with the Führer – only he can authorize their use.'

Walter went to the giant wall map and looked at the positions of the reported parachute landings. Were they a feint for a real one in the Pas de Calais area?

They were over a very wide area indeed. There must be hundreds of them – no, thousands, if you allowed that for every one detected there must be many more undiscovered.

But in Normandy?

Surely there would have been sightings of an invasion fleet over such a wide stretch of the channel by now? This couldn't really be the start of it, could it?

As they kitted up Robbie thought of the letter he'd written to Maddie and left on his bedside cabinet. Had he finished it properly? He was so tired and confused by the overuse of Benzedrine that now he was worried that he might have just sealed it up without properly signing off.

There was a light rain when they were driven out in the dark to the Typhoons, but it stopped almost as soon as they were dropped off the back of the Hillman trucks.

He settled himself in the cockpit, the rigger having helped him with his parachute and connections. The signal came for engine start, and the night was split by the deafening, awesome, roar of the 2000 h.p. Napier engines.

Soon the CO was leading out the line of Typhoons, navigation lights on, and turning into the flare path. His voice came over the R/T.

'Poker aircraft, line-astern climb in sections, reform at cloud tops – climb on heading 250.'

In turn, they followed the CO's exhaust flame between the gooseneck flares and lifted off into the night sky.

Robbie felt the now accustomed tremendous surge of power as he opened the throttle. In seconds he was in thin cloud, amid navigation lights glowing brightly in the swirling mist and rain, then he was breaking out into a starlit sky where the moon was riding between great peaks of hurrying clouds. They switched off the navigation lights.

As they flew on he looked all around, up and then down, just as somebody else broke R/T silence, he must have left his radio on transmit.

'Phew! Look at that.'

Down below on the silvery sea he could see the dark shapes and white wakes of ships, thousands upon thousands of them. The invasion fleet was filling the seascape below all the way to the horizon in every direction.

It was an awe-inspiring sight.

John Fairfax had no idea of the passage of time, but suddenly he got mad. Had he trained all those years, just to end up a shivering mess in a ditch?

In the dark he shook his head, found his water bottle, and took a swig to clean his mouth.

Suddenly he heard a movement. He sank back to earth and used his cricket, just the once. A double click followed.

In his relief he almost stood up straight and called out, but some animal caution stopped him. Instead he hissed into the night 'flash.'

A voice said: 'I've forgotten the fuckin' reply.'

It was wonderful, hearing an American voice.

He called back 'You're supposed to say "thunder".'

'Oh yeah, then "welcome", right?'

He waited, gun ready, until he saw a silhouette near him. The helmet was American.

'Am I glad to see you, Lieutenant.'

He recognized the man and slapped him on the shoulder.

'And you too, Cohen.'

'Have you seen anybody else, sir?'

He thought of the dead trooper.

'No.'

Cohen's helmet shook from side to side in disbelief.

'What a fuckin' mess. Where the hell are we?'

John Fairfax eased his chinstrap.

'Your guess is as good as mine. Come on, I thought I saw a barn this way.'

Crouching, they moved slowly along either side of the lane, pausing every time the moon rode clear of the clouds and bathed everything in shades of blue on black. The night smelt of the summer countryside. It had gone unbelievably quiet, except for the sound of a nightingale.

Minutes passed as they edged their way carefully along, until John thought he saw movement further down the lane, but once more the clouds obscured the moon.

He sank down, hissing a warning to Cohen. There were shapes, two – no, three, maybe even four. They waited, eyes straining in the darkness, fingers on triggers.

Sounds of muffled footsteps and heavy breathing drew nearer. His heart was pounding so violently he thought they must hear it.

Slowly he raised his tin cricket and pressed just the once. The sound was like a pistol shot.

There was a scuffling sound, and then silence resumed, no answering *click-clack.*

Sweating, he began to tighten his finger on the trigger.

'Moo.'

Cohen's hard Bronx accent cut through the night air. 'Fuckin' cows, I nearly shot a fuckin' cow.'

The animals, spooked by the sudden voice, panicked and rushed headlong past them, shouldering John Fairfax into the ditch.

He'd just climbed out, was on his knees trying to find his Garand as Cohen reached him, when there was a burst of Schmeiser machinegunfire and a fiery boom as a grenade went off a couple of hundred yards away.

They both rolled back into the ditch as the mutilated cows bellowed and screamed in agony, that lasted all of a minute before the firing stopped.

Beside John, Cohen whispered.

'Krauts.'

John Fairfax didn't need to confirm it, as the guttural sound of Germans talking to each other drew nearer.

The moon rode free again. They watched in frozen disbelief as a five-man patrol filed past and disappeared once more into the night as the veil of darkness descended.

They had been so close they could have tapped the nearest man on the ankles.

Cohen hissed: 'Shit, sir, we had 'em. We could'a taken them out – all of 'em.'

But John Fairfax had been unable to pull the trigger to actually kill five men. If Cohen had opened up there was no doubt that he would have followed, but to start the killing. . . . It would have felt like cold-blooded murder.

Frightened by his lack of action, that he'd failed at the first hurdle, he said brusquely: 'We need to keep going.'

They'd been moving for ten minutes when a loud click rooted them to the spot.

Cohen answered with a double click.

A voice said, 'Flash.'

John Fairfax answered 'Thunder.'

Yet another voice, to the right of the first said 'Hundred and First?'

Tensely Fairfax replied, 'OK, you group, come on out.'

From the shadows three men emerged, their carbines still raised.

He was the only officer.

In the next hour they found another five live troopers, and several dead ones.

He waited whilst they cut a body down from a tree; the man had broken his neck.

Two more corpses were found at a crossroads, when one of the men tripped over them in the road.

They had been shot, their blood was making great black pools in the beams of their flashlights.

'Looks like they were unarmed, sir, and had no helmets. They must have been prisoners.'

It did something to him.

He looked around at the green-and-black camouflaged young faces, where only the whites of the troopers' eyes showed, and knew they were relying on him.

'We came to do a job. Let's do it.'

# CHAPTER THIRTY

The Brigadeführer gathered them all around a map table. 'From all the reports the paratroop landing is widespread, therefore it's a considerable force, not a feint.'

'But sir, how can we be sure?' asked a Sturmannführer.

The Brigadeführer gestured at the table.

'Look for yourself. There have been skirmishes here, here, here – even here.'

He thumped the table every time he pointed to a place.

A Standartenführer wondered about any sightings at sea.

'None, but there have been no Luftwaffe overflights of the area – won't be till dawn – nor over the Pas de Calais.'

He paused, frowned.

'But surely – the weather? The sea is too rough for a seaborne operation – it would be madness.'

The meteorological officer coughed.

'Winds are abating, sir. For the next twenty-four hours there will be milder conditions before we expect the weather to turn stormy again.'

The Brigadeführer grunted, shook his head.

'That doesn't give them the chance to reinforce their initial landings. I don't know what to think.'

Just then a Sturmmann arrived, mudstained and soaking.

He threw a salute.

The Brigadeführer frowned.

'You have news, Sturmmann?'

'Sir.'

The man turned as two privates carried in a squat dummy shaped and dressed in the camouflage uniform of an Allied paratrooper. Its parachute, bundled up, was still attached.

'What in God's heaven is that?'

They set it down on the floor as the Sturmmann explained.

'These have been found over a wide area, sir.'

He indicated several soot-stained holes.

'On impact it fired off blanks for several minutes.'

The Brigadeführer exploded.

'My God! – It *is* a feint. The real landing must be coming in the Calais area.'

Walter frowned.

Perhaps that was what the enemy wanted them to think?

The dawn broke, the sky grew lighter and the stars disappeared as they reched the very end of their patrol. Then the leader's voice crackled in his ear.

'We have trade, chaps, advised by Blackgang Radar – nine plus, fifteen miles north. Opening up.'

They increased to maximum cruise as Robbie's eyes automatically checked his fuel level. After two minutes they went into a shallow dive to achieve tactical advantage.

He saw them at the same time as a voice broke R/T silence.

'There – two miles ahead and below, sir, look like one-nineties.'

'Got 'em.'

With their increased speed the range closed quickly.

'Right, boys. Tally ho!'

With that the leader dropped a wing and led them down on to the gaggle of dark specks.

The enemy suddenly saw them coming and broke violently apart. Exhaust smoke flared from boosters and vapour streamed from the wingtips as they pulled hard away.

Robbie dived after one with a yellow spinner; it twisted and turned as it did everything to get away, then it made the mistake of climbing.

The 'Tiffy' responded with a huge surge of power as Robbie put her into a zoom climb at full throttle, and closed to within 300 yards.

He slid the safety off, his gloved hand lightly covering the firing tit.

Suddenly, he was closing so fast that he had to throttle back.

When the 190 pilot realized he could not out-climb his attacker, he rolled over into a diving turn. Robbie fired a short burst just ahead of the yellow spinner, and saw the enemy fly into the tracer.

Strikes appeared on the fuselage and on the wing. White coolant streamed back, followed by oily black smoke and then licks of flame.

Before he could put in another burst, his head was filled with his wingman's screaming voice: 'Break left! Break left!'

Robbie tramped the rudder bar and wrenched the yoke over. He blacked out for a second, just fleetingly he caught a glimpse of another 190, a swastika on its fuselage, as it flashed past – then he was in cloud.

The R/T became a confusion of yells.

'Look out, Jimmy – on your tail.'

'Bandits above, watch out.'

'Christ Jack – Jack. . . .'

He broke out of the cloud, found himself above a 190, and rolled straight into the attack, but it had already seen him, and it disappeared back into the cloud.

The danger of a collision in the mêlée was now great, and the smell of cordite in the cockpit seemed to be worse. His wingman confirmed his fears.

'You've got a hole in your belly just behind the wing root.'

Robbie checked his instruments and controls. All seemed normal but he radioed he'd been hit and was making for home.

There was 100 miles of English Channel to cross. Under the guidance of Control he headed for the nearest point on the coast accompanied by his wingman, and settled back at a low cruising speed, constantly checking his fuel, oil and coolant. All seemed well. To his relief the cliffs of the West Country appeared at last.

They turned and flew along the south coast. He was aware of the ships to his starboard, still hundreds of them, crossing and now recrossing the grey sea. And he could see the gunfire flashes of battle flickering continually on the French side.

He wondered how it was going.

# CHAPTER THIRTY-ONE

The fighting, when it came, happened with brutal suddenness. The light was shining in the eastern sky when a German suddenly rose from behind a hedgerow and shouted: '*Hande hoch*,' then instantly opened fire cutting the lead man almost in two.

John Fairfax fired his first round in anger, and killed his first man even as he threw himself to the ground.

A 'potato-masher', the long handled German grenade hit the asphalt as he rolled away.

There was a blinding explosion and a blast of gravel, and then guns were firing from every angle. The fierce fight only ended when John Fairfax suddenly pulled himself up and shouted: 'Come on – come on!'

In that split second he had no idea what had got into him, or whether the others would follow.

But follow they did.

Throwing grenades and firing their carbines they stormed the hedgerow where they found four dead Germans. Others were fleeing into the dawn.

He sank to his haunches, began to shiver, tried to light a cigarette, but his hand was shaking too much.

A lighter appeared and with difficulty he held the tip of the cigarette in the flame until it was alight.

As he drew in the smoke he looked up at the smiling yellow-and-black face of Cohen, whose helmet was pushed back off his forehead.

'Well done, Lieutenant,' said Cohen.

Fairfax tried a grin back, but guessed it failed.

They didn't know it, but isolated skirmishes like theirs had been going on all night.

The German High Command was flooded with reports of actions over a huge area.

The mood had changed again.

Some American prisoners had been taken, so there had been a real attack, not just diversionary dummies.

The exchanges around the map table became more heated with the frustration of indecision.

It was then that Walter Raus remembered the detachment of three tanks from his regiment, and a couple of Scout cars. They had been sent to Normandy as part of the ongoing training programme to acclimatize themselves with the terrain in all the regions in which they might have to fight.

It wasn't much, but they could report the situation as they found it at first hand.

The Brigadeführer was delighted.

'Excellent. Get on to them, have them probe towards the coast.'

He looked at his watch, swung around.

'To hell with the blackout, open the curtains. I want to know as soon as it's light.'

The mess tent was noisy with the excited chatter of pilots exchanging stories, some illustrated with hands miming aircraft, wheeling and diving. Others were gathered around the adjutant and some intelligence officers, eager for news of the landings.

Robbie listened, but he didn't feel anything. All he wanted to do was to get on a train and get to Maddie. He wanted Maddie, with a sudden urgency.

He picked at his food, then pushed it away, strolled outside, lit a cigarette. The field was alive with aircraft taking off and landing, others were being swarmed over by mechanics. Allied air supremacy was now total over north-west France, and really over all of occupied Europe.

Only over the Reich itself were the great armadas of Allied fighters and bombers still being challenged by the increasingly desperate fighters of the Luftwaffe, including, it was said, a new fast propellerless jet. But with the second European front now opened and heavy fighting in Russia and Italy, surely the war couldn't last much longer? Germany was like a boxer on the ropes, albeit a still dangerous opponent.

His thoughts were interrupted by a loudspeaker calling his squadron to the ops room.

He dropped the remains of the cigarette and ground it out with his boot. His stomach knotted with the usual fear and excited anticipation of the unknown.

He was walking with a group when one of them pointed.

'Over there.'

He turned, screwed his eyes up against the low sunlight.

He heard it before he saw it, the interrupted stutter of a Typhoon engine. When he saw the plane his chest tightened. It had joined the circuit, one wheel down, the other fully retracted, and the canopy was only half-open.

They watched in horror, knowing that the man would never land safely, that as soon as it touched down it would dig into the ground. He should have climbed, and parachuted out, but no doubt the canopy was jammed. The poor sod must be sweating it out, knowing that there was no hope.

The Typhoon's wheel scraped the ground, and then it slewed around, the wing digging in. Instantly it was a massive ball of flame spewing along the runway as the high-octane fuel exploded.

Then there was silence as clouds of black oily smoke drifted in a great pall over the field. There were no exploded cannon shells; he must have used them all up.

Slowly Robbie was aware of bells ringing. He saw the meat wagon and the fire engine racing out, even as other Typhoons, low on fuel and with pilots drained of energy, continued to land.

Later, when he came out of the intelligence tent he saw four firemen, two in flameproof asbestos suits carrying something in a blanket.

The bile came up into his throat.

# CHAPTER THIRTY-TWO

The man on point suddenly raised his arm. Instantly they sank down.

For the last hour, with men continually coming out of the hedgerows and joining them, they had moved through the countryside as daylight began to flood the deep dark lanes of the bocage. In the distance came the continual deep booming of naval guns. The invasion was imminent.

With information gleaned from the others John Fairfax had decided that one of the causeways that they had to seize to stop any German counter-attack on the 4th Infantry coming off Utah beach was only a few miles away.

Cohen, crouching, hurried forward, hunkered down beside him.

'What is it, sir?'

'Listen.'

There was a low hill before them, and almost immediately he could hear the clanking sound and engine roar of tracked vehicles.

Fairfax frowned. 'Tanks?' There was nothing in the intelligence reports about panzers in the area.

'Could be half-tracks, sir.'

John Fairfax turned and signalled the rest of the men to scatter and take cover.

In seconds the lane looked empty. The sound of movement ceased, then the engines turned off. They could hear shouts in German.

Fairfax whispered to the point man.

'Come on, let's take a look.'

On their bellies they crawled to the top of the rise, carefully raised their heads.

The trooper whistled softly under his breath.

'Jesus – panzers.'

Before them were three tanks and several trucks disgorging soldiers in field grey, who were assembling loosely in platoons. Cigarettes were being lit. Several officers were consulting maps.

The tank crews were getting out, stretching their legs and relieving themselves where they stood.

They were dressed in black fatigues.

John Fairfax grunted.

'They're SS; the others are regular Wehrmacht. Looks like they're a scratch bunch, maybe put together in a hurry.'

Then his eyes took in the land beyond the halted column. There, in front of them, was the elevated causeway leading through the deliberately flooded fields.

It was one of the targets they had come to seize, but they should have been in at least battalion strength, with anti-tank weapons.

Instead, they were around thirty strong and lightly armed.

'What are we going to do, sir?'

He felt the presence of past Fairfaxes looking down on him, heard their voices in his head.

'We've got to put those tanks out of action.'

The trooper looked at him in amazement.

'How are we going to do that, sir?'

John Fairfax gave another grunt.

'We've got surprise on our side. We'll rush them – disable them with Gammon grenades.'

The man grinned.

'Easy-peasy, Lieutenant. Sure got a fire in your belly.'

They crawled back to the nest.

He briefed them quickly, grimly aware that the 'fire' was not going to be there for ever, and ended with what he hoped was a morale-boosting.

'OK, so fix bayonets and give 'em hell.'

They crawled back to the top of the rise, spreading out, all eyes on him. When he was satisfied that they were ready he took a deep breath, conscious that it was now or never. He had one last fleeting thought of Sally before he stood up, legs shaking, and yelled: 'Come on.'

The troopers rose as one and stormed forward, howling like banshees.

Taken completely by surprise, the Germans had no idea of the size of the force attacking them out of the darkness of the retreating night.

Some ran straight away, most just stood unmoving for several vital seconds: enough time for the lead troopers to reach them – and the tanks.

Suddenly jolted into action, a commander leapt back on to his turret. John Fairfax shot him off as another paratrooper pulled the pin and palmed a grenade through the driver's aperture.

But by now German officers had rallied their men. The fighting was savage, with bullet and bayonet, knife and hands, and lasted minutes before the German line broke. The attackers stood, chests heaving, shocked by their own violence.

They had managed to reach a second tank, blowing off one of its tracks, but the third had gone into reverse, raking the men heading for it with machinegun fire, cutting them all down.

Now its main barrel rotated, then lowered.

Somebody yelled: 'Shit shit shit! Take cover.'

They hit the ground, John Fairfax trying with all his might to sink into the very earth itself.

There was a sharp crack, a whine, then the earth punched them in the face. With a roar a column of dirt shot into the air, then stones and branches came raining down. The man next to him was screaming: non-stop, screaming. His legs were bloody stumps above the knees.

Something came over John Fairfax, something primitive. Almost without thinking he leapt up, ran straight at the tank.

Two other men rose and followed, firing from the hip and yelling like the madmen they were.

The tank's machinegun ripped the life from the other two as they reached the driver's hatch.

Crying with rage, John Fairfax scrambled up the side and found the top hatch open. He stuck the barrel of the Garand in and loosed off a continuous round, hearing the bullets ricocheting around the steel interior.

There was a muffled sound and a sob. He pulled the pin from a grenade, dropped it in, and rolled away.

The explosion was soft, like a low *whump*, then thick black smoke poured from the hatch as though from a chimney. The driver started screaming, but somebody shot him.

Fairfax looked around. The field was theirs.

Hurriedly he organized high-explosive satchels to be placed in the other two tanks. The men scrambled into ditches before the explosions ripped the leaves from the trees. One tank blew up into pieces, its turret flying high into the air. The ammunition in the others erupted in great orange flames and flying ordnance, like pyrotechnics, as the armament fired off.

When the worst of the explosions ceased Fairfax wondered who it was who was sobbing beside him.

Then he realized it was himself.

# CHAPTER THIRTY-THREE

The sky had lightened outside the windows, and by the time Walter Raus had stepped outside to clear his head from the frenzied activity that seemed to be going nowhere, the rooks in the trees near the private chapel were joining in the morning chorus.

The new day had now well and truly dawned, and by the time he had taken some deep lungfuls of the beautiful fresh air of the French countryside, and gone back in through the ornate hall, stopping only to relieve himself and have the attendant brush his uniform jacket, the news had hardened.

An invasion fleet was off the coast of Normandy, and landings had been reported.

By midday it appeared the enemy had a bridgehead a couple of miles deep in places. Walter was restless. He knew that Rommel wanted any invasion force swept back into the sea before the Allies could get established.

But the headquarters of Army Group B took the view that it was not yet disastrous. Despite the Führer's continued reluctance to commit the panzers, the Allied air superiority was such that their early release would undoubtedly have resulted in severe losses even before they were anywhere near the beachheads.

News had come in from the training detachment that they had moved to engage some of the American paratroop force, but there were no details yet.

Walter poured over the maps with the others, all eager to get on the move, to enter the battle as soon as possible.

Rommel, who had been with his family in Bavaria, was now on his way to his headquarters, and was expected to arrive later that evening to take charge of the fragmented command structure.

Walter Raus let out a sigh and shook his head.

'At last, we will get clear orders.'

They went reluctantly into lunch in the elegant eighteenth-century dining room, sitting at the long polished table set with silver and fine porcelain.

The steward held the silver tureen as Walter Raus ladled soup into his bowl. He was too much of a seasoned campaigner not to eat, though he was far too on edge to be hungry.

When he'd served on the Eastern Front, he had gone days with only a lump of black bread. You soon learnt that food was fuel. Their tanks couldn't run without it, neither could they.

Afterwards he went out to his section bunkered in the woods, and returned the salute of a young tank commander.

They ducked under the camouflage netting that prevented the fighter-bombers of the enemy from seeing them.

Satisfied that everything was ready for an immediate move when the order was given, he started to make his way back when the warning klaxon started its wail.

He leapt into the nearest slit trench as the 88mm flak guns opened up a murderous barrage, peppering the sky with thousands of bursts of orange turning to black puffs of smoke.

The single-engined fighters came in low just above the treetops, flying in twos, six in all, releasing 500lb bombs.

The earth shook and dirt and leaves ripped and rained down.

It was all over in seconds.

Walter climbed out, dusted himself off and looked around.

A dark column of black oily smoke was rising above the trees. It looked as though the fuel dump had been hit.

Fortunately, it had been almost empty, all the tanks, half-tracks, self-propelled guns and trucks had been refuelled ready for their deployment.

All the same, it showed what they would be up against.

He knew the enemy aircraft had been Typhoons, with their hated and feared shape, and red, white and blue roundels.

These planes also had big black and white stripes on their wings. He wondered if that was significant – to do with the invasion?

He paced back to the château, and was climbing the steps of the main entrance when a Sturmmann came running out, saw him and drew himself up.

'Sir, movement orders.'

Walter Raus quickened his pace. At last they were going into action.

They had trained up the eighteen- and nineteen-year-olds, and now they were ready.

He realized that in reality they would have only one chance, despite ideas of defensive lines, but after that it would be a war of attrition – and the Allies had unlimited supplies – of both men and materials.

He knew Rommel was right.

It was now or never.

Just before they moved out, with the roar of engines and shouts and clatter of the men boarding the trucks making it difficult to hear, a signaller ran up, saluted, and handed him a message sheet.

It was terse and to the point.

Their detachment of three tanks had been in action against airborne forces. None had survived.

Walter Raus balled the paper up and threw it away as whistles blew.

He stood up, raised his arm, and waved his columns forward.

As he sat down again, he wondered at the nature of the battle they were about to undertake.

The Americans seemed to be better than everyone thought.

# CHAPTER THIRTY-FOUR

Maddie woke early and washed her hair before getting to the Academy at nine o'clock. On Tuesdays she had a long day, starting with composition.

When she wandered into the small lecture room at a quarter past, the other students were already there, lounging around and talking to each other.

When the lecturer eventually arrived he look flustered as he laid his briefcase on a table.

'I'm sorry I'm late, all the trains from the south coast are running late, more than usual. There's quite widespread disruption.'

They swung around, facing him as he set out his papers. Then he went to the blackboard and started chalking up some headings.

Just as he turned back to address them the door flew open and an excited secretary stood there.

'Come quickly, all of you, come on.'

Bewildered, they scrambled up after her. The sirens hadn't gone off, had they?

The staff common room was packed with people, students and staff alike, gathered around a large wireless.

'What is it?' asked Maddie.

'The programme was stopped and an announcer said to "stand by",' was the answer.

There could only be one thing this important, surely, unless something had happened to Churchill?

The wireless crackled into life.

*This is the BBC Home Service – and here is a special bulletin read by John Snagge.*

There was a pause in which people shot worried glances at each other.

*D-Day has come. Early this morning the Allies began the assault on the north-western face of Hitler's European fortress.*

She hardly heard the rest. The jubilation after so many long weary years of war was spontaneous; they could hear cheering out in the street.

The radio said the King was going to speak to the nation at nine o'clock that night.

But all Maddie could think of was Robbie.

Later she was on the top deck of a bus looking down at the crowds of people gathered around the newsvendor's desk, the headlines **D-DAY** and **SECOND FRONT** in huge black type on their displays.

Newspapers were selling like hot cakes.

From her position she could see the excitement, hear it around her as people crashed up and down the metal stairs and swung into nearby seats, talking of how the war was nearly over.

How could they be so foolish? Nobody knew yet what was happening – it could be a disaster.

Then she relented. After years of bad news, of suffering, people were eager for it to come to an end.

She got off at her stop. It was a short walk to the church hall where they were preparing a concert for the people of the East End.

The King was going to broadcast to the nation that night at nine o'clock. She wondered whether they would halt the concert while it happened, perhaps put it on a public address system?

At the street corner was a red pillar box. She slipped out the letter, kissed it again on the sealed down flap on which she had put in block capitals S.W.A.L.K. – sealed with a loving kiss. She knew it was daft, but couldn't help herself.

For a second she held it in the opening, then let it go, hearing it flutter down inside.

What would he think when he opened it and read what she had written? She could remember it word for word: that she had some wonderful news. She was his wife now in every way except the actual ceremony, because she was carrying their first child, yes, wasn't it wonderful!

*Darling, I can't wait to see you again. I still look the same Robbie, it takes time to show, you know, but there is a part of* you *growing inside me, so we truly are together now – for ever.*

She felt her eyes moisten as she thought yet again of the never-ending miracle that was taking place within her.

Later she went to church, lit a candle, prayed; something she hadn't done for a long time. She repeated over and over, 'Please God, may he be all right – please God, may he be all right. Please take care of him – please.'

Sally looked around the large room. It was a scene of intense activity, with dispatch riders coming and going, and plotters before a huge situation map of the entire area in Normandy, with arrows showing the landings on Juno, Sword, Gold, Omaha and Utah beaches.

Groups of anxious, and in some cases, fearful-looking senior officers were talking earnestly before it.

In the middle of the night before last, she had been transferred to the Supreme Headquarters, Allied Expeditionary Force – SHAEF for short, at Southwick House near Portsmouth – more staff had been needed to cover illness.

Ike was there, with Monty and other top brass.

As she moved among the desks, giving out the latest signals, she glanced up at the map.

What was attracting all the worried looks was the area marked 'Omaha'.

Whereas all the other beaches' arrows indicated movement inland, the arrow on 'Omaha' remained resolutely stuck at the waterline.

She wondered what was going on there – going badly wrong, she presumed.

But her attention was really focused on the unit signs inland, indicating the landing zones of the British paratroopers to the east, and the American 82$^{nd}$ and 101$^{st}$ airborne divisions to the centre and west. It was difficult to glean any information on what had happened – was happening, though she had heard that British gliders had seized a vital bridge.

Although they had never talked about it, she knew that John must be in the thick of it somewhere over there; she began to feel sick, but was kept far too busy to dwell on it. As the hours passed the tension and sense of foreboding over what was happening on Omaha became almost unbearable. The room became thick with cigarette smoke.

The first aerial pictures of the beachheads were brought in, taken by a photo-reconnaissance aircraft.

There was a great gathering of senior officers around the large black-and-white photographs that had been sent over by motorcycle dispatch rider from RAF Benson, where the photographs had been interpreted.

What was causing the commanders to look so shocked was what appeared to be skeins of dark oil on the beach at the waterline.

But it was not oil.

They had been interpreted as blood.

There was a massacre going on at Omaha.

# CHAPTER THIRTY-FIVE

Robbie stood on the wing and looked about him. The rest of the pilots were either climbing in, or still walking around their aircraft, checking control surfaces.

He settled down into his cockpit, smelling the usual whiff of high-octane fuel, rubber, paint – and vomit. His stomach cramped a little with the knowledge of what was to come.

After his checks he signalled for engine start. The propeller gave a slow flick around as the cartridge in the starter fired, and then with a cough of oily exhaust smoke the 24-cylinder engine exploded into life and the propeller disappeared into a blur.

All around the field the other engines burst into life, blasting air and deafening the ground crews.

Mechanics sat or hung on to wing tips to balance the shuddering Typhoons.

With his cockpit checks completed he opened the radiator flap and waved the chocks away. Satisfied that all was clear he released the brake lever. One by one the other Typhoons were swinging their tails from side to side as they moved forward, queuing up at the end of the runway.

He watched the CO go first, followed by others. Then he was rumbling forward under full power, bumping and thumping until just the tail lifted. Then, as he clawed into the air, he became aware of the smoothness of flight.

Robbie got the undercarriage up, hearing and feeling the wheels thud into their wells. He saw the green light come on.

They formed into flights and headed out over the Channel.

The briefing had been to the point. Enemy panzer units were now beginning to head for the invasion beaches. They were to be stopped at all costs.

At 15,000 feet they passed over the beaches and swept on, turning into a new course under the orders of control. Half an hour later they flew over a line of grey shapes on a straight road running through a wood.

The airwaves crackled with shouts just as, all along the convoy, a line of winking red and yellow flashes erupted.

It was flak guns opening up on them. Straight away the CO started to lead them round and back. They split into fours and began to dive down all along the convoy's length.

Robbie could see soldiers in black and field grey running for the cover of the trees as the Typhoons began their dives. Flak wagons began sending up a deadly stream of tracer.

Robbie watched his own cannon-fire strike a petrol bowser, which blew up in a mass of yellow flame and black smoke.

As he climbed away he saw more aircraft arriving, Tempests with tank-busting rockets. It was like a sharks' feeding-frenzy.

The sky was now dangerously full of diving climbing aircraft and the radio was alive with shouts and warnings.

'Bandits.'

Robbie looked up, his heart coming into his mouth.

More Me109s than he had seen for a long time were coming down on them.

He immediately boosted the Typhoon into a tight climb to meet them head on, as others did the same. Then everything happened at the usual fast and furious pace. He got off a burst at one of the slim, smaller enemy aircraft, then found a line of tracer passing his port wing.

He broke off and dived into the nearest cloud. When he came out the sky was empty – he had never got used to that, but there was no sign of either a British or German fighter in the sky.

Keeping a continuous eye out he turned for home, flying along the shattered burning convoy. The Tempests had struck; great columns of black smoke rose from several tanks and mingled with the still blazing fuel wagons. It was no longer the immensely strong formation it had been, and it would be seriously short of fuel.

John Fairfax was now part of a force of several hundred, and they had been battling on for over two days, linking up, and making thrusts to try and join with the 29$^{th}$ Division from Omaha.

But German paratroops had engaged them in a fierce hand-to-hand battle in the heavily wooded and hedgerowed bocage, forcing their advance to a snail's pace, then to a complete halt. And all the time they were aware that it was a race against time, because the Germans would be bringing up the dreaded panzer divisions.

In a ditch, with the enemy barely seventy yards away, he fell into a deep sleep as others watched for any movement.

Occasionally bursts from Schmeiser machineguns ripped through the hedges, sending branches and leaves fluttering down like the fall on to his stinking, aching body.

But his exhaustion was bone deep, he didn't even stir.

Over everything was the stench of death. The swollen bodies of dead cows were everywhere.

An hour later rations were brought in by men crawling on their bellies, dragging the packs behind them. It was midday, and even the sound of the naval bombardment had died away to a distant rumble.

'Sir . . . sir.'

He was shaken into a sudden startled, consciousness, jerking his Garand up until he saw the PFC before him.

'Sir – chow.'

He sank back and took the proffered rations. He didn't immediately eat, but lay looking up at the blue sky. Far away he could see the vapour trails of high flying bombers heading back to England.

It seemed a lifetime since he'd walked on the beaches of Cornwall with Sally. He pictured her, with the Atlantic wind blowing her hair around her face, cheeks flushed and rosy – but back in Maine.

Another burst of machinegun fire brought him back to reality. He ripped open the chow packet, began forcing in the food, wolfing it down in case he was interrupted by the Krauts. His mother wouldn't have appreciated his manners.

As he finished and took a swig of water from his flask a colonel and a major came crawling past.

The former flicked a finger to the brim of his steel helmet in answer to John Fairfax's salute.

'Lieutenant, we're going to take another crack at reaching Carentan – there's not much time left. The Krauts have got tanks only twenty miles away. Get your men ready. We move out in ten minutes.'

He crawled away as John Fairfax beckoned to his first sergeant.

The time for daydreaming was over.

# CHAPTER THIRTY-SIX

Once again Walter Raus got to his feet, brushing off the twigs and mud as the engines of the British aircraft – Typhoons – faded away.

He looked around at the burning trucks and the dying men scattered on the road. Others were on their feet, cursing and shaking with the effect of the murderous blasts of cannon and rockets.

Quickly he started barking orders, getting the dead pulled to the side as the medics tended to the screaming, groaning wounded, some with bellies ripped open, blue, glistening intestines spilling out. He doubted if they would survive. Most were not yet twenty years old.

With the crash and screech of metal on metal the tanks began bulldozing the wrecks to one side, so that the convoy could continue its dash.

But they were suffering heavy casualties, and were severely delayed. In the last few days they'd lost forty petrol tankers, nearly ninety trucks and half-tracks and six tanks to the continuous attacks from the air.

At last they were now only a few kilometres from Carentan. If they could reach the village and reinforce it, the link up of the Americans from the different beaches could be prevented, and then the thrust to push the invasion back into the sea could begin.

He scrambled up on to the seat of his Kubel open-topped scout car and, as soon as the vehicles ahead of him started to move he raised his hand and waved them forward.

He dropped down into his seat and looked warily around the sky. Although the British must know that they had badly mauled them, they would be back for more. The soldiers had removed the doors on many of the vehicles so that they could get out as quickly as possible, and many of them lay on the front mudguards, looking upwards, scanning the sky.

The convoy got up to speed led by motorcycle combinations that took it in turn to stop all traffic at crossroads and wave them in the right direction. As the scout car bumped and shuddered over the badly repaired road Raus was acutely aware that the last time he had fought in France, during the Blitzkrieg, the air had been ruled by the Luftwaffe, their advance preceded by the Stuka dive-bombers with their terrifying sirens sounding as they dived on to every position.

He grunted. But the Allies had learnt the lesson. The boot was now well and truly on the other foot.

The thought of France back then, in that wonderful summer of 1940, revived good memories. After the campaign they had taken bread, cheese and wine, picnicking in the glorious hot weather, playing football and swimming in the cool rivers, watching the red ball of the sun sinking over the fields of cut and stooked wheat.

The whine of a diving aircraft brought him back to the present with terrifying speed. He sprang to his feet, one hand gripping the windscreen as he waved with the other towards a wood they were passing.

'Take cover, take cover.'

Sally was on duty without relief for two days.

Exhausted, she was eventually released just before midnight along with three other WRNS. In her room she kicked off her shoes and lay down on her bunk, pulling her tie loose. She would change and get ready for bed in a few minutes, but just for the moment her mind was racing with thoughts of the momentous times she, along with all the people of the free world, had just lived through.

But, unlike them, she had shared the roller-coaster of emotions, the sheer finger-biting tension of the early hours, especially the tragedy, almost a disaster of Omaha, where the initial landing had met murderous fire, and had faltered, sustaining heavy casualties. Only by heroic self-sacrifice and sheer determination, had the beach been finally taken. Even now, by the time she was relieved of duty there was no clear indication of what was happening behind the beachheads, where John must be. There were many reports of individual actions, of the exits from the beaches being finally secured, but other objectives, like some of the inland villages and crossroads still remained in German hands. They had been prime targets of the paratroopers. There had been no word of the casualty rate for the airborne forces.

During the day she had been forced to put thoughts of John to the back of her mind, but now her anxiety mushroomed.

Sally took a deep breath and got control of herself.

From her brown case under her bed she took out a framed photo that he had given her. It showed him with his mother and father, taken just before he had left home, in his uniform, smiling into the lens, arms around them both. She looked at it for some time, then gently pressed her lips to his face. She was still gazing at it as her eyelids fluttered, closed and her hand slowly released its hold on the photograph. It stayed on her chest, rising and falling as she breathed, until she turned on her side. It slid off, fell to the floor, face down.

After another seventy-two hours Sally was at last replaced from her stint at Southwick House. She was given a week's leave in the expectation that if the invasion and second front continued as planned, SHAEF headquarters would transfer to France, and follow the front line across Europe.

Although she was thrilled to have been selected, she was desperate for news of John. It overshadowed everything.

She did not leave the grounds of Southwick House. Twice a day, every day, she went to a phone, waiting impatiently while she was connected. When she eventually got through to a friend in the operations room she was told – no, no word about John, or his unit, but information was still only slowly coming out of the confused and disorganized situation of the airborne drop.

# CHAPTER THIRTY-SEVEN

Maddie was sick: it happened every morning now. As she reached up and pulled the chain, flushing the lavatory, she wondered whether it was time to tell them at the academy: and more to the point, her mother. The latter would be shattered, not only because of her Catholic faith, which had sustained her through her troubled life, but because Maddie had seemingly ruined her career, after so much sacrifice. Even Maddie had yet to come to terms with what had happened.

In the kitchen she filled a glass of water and swilled out her mouth. Then she went back into the sitting room and switched on the wireless for the early-morning news, dreading to hear whether there was any worrying information about the RAF.

There was. Apparently there had been bombing raids in support of the Allied army – nothing more, but it was enough to bring back her queasiness She rushed back to the lavatory.

By the time she reached the academy she felt better, and put off telling them – yet again. But she could not do so much longer, and had no idea what would happen when she did.

When she got home that night she was utterly bushed. It was all she could do to change for bed. Wearing her dressing-gown she made a cup of cocoa and took it into the sitting room.

Curled up with her feet beneath her, she pulled the writing pad and fountain pen that were lying on the seat beside her on to her lap.

She decided to tackle the letter to home before she wrote to Robbie, telling them about him – and the baby. She knew she would tell a lot of white lies: it was easier. She would say she'd known him for months, that he was already taking instruction from a priest in the air force – oh, and he wasn't English! But in truth what she most feared was how her father would react.

When it was done she had a sip of her drink, contemplated the new empty page before her, then began to write.

*My Dearest Sweetest Robbie*
*I hurt so badly because you are not with me. Darling, do you love me the same way? Without you I am incomplete – have I said that before? Forgive me if I have, but it's true. Every minute of every hour since you went I've been more and more aware of how much I love you, and need you.*

*Darling, take care of yourself – for me and our baby. Please don't do anything silly.*

Even as she was writing she guessed he was most probably doing something she wouldn't care to think about.

Inge had heard the rumour: the Allies had landed in France. There had been no official communication, but the hospital grapevine was full of it. Somebody's son who worked at army headquarters, the OKW had passed the word to his brother, a medical orderly in the Luftwaffe, who in turn had told his girlfriend, a nurse who worked on one of the wards. All over Berlin the word was spreading; you could see the furtive talking going on at any street corner, the apprehension in the looks of women chatting in the food queues.

She didn't, like many of her fellow citizens, she supposed, know whether to be happy or sad.

Sad for herself, because Walter would again be in the thick of any fighting, and for others, not only herself, because it was another nail in the coffin of the Fatherland.

But she knew that there would be many who would be relieved: wanting, if there was to be defeat – though nobody talked openly like that – to be overrun by the American and British, not the Asiatic hordes from Communist Russia. Surely the Führer would never allow that to happen?

She got on with helping an elderly patient into a wheelchair to take him down to the basement shelter for the night. There was nothing she could do to help her husband but pray, and even that would have to wait.

Robbie Cochran lay on his cot, not asleep, not smoking, not doing anything, just staring up at the canvas of the tent roof.

But he was thinking, had been thinking for most of the night, his thoughts going round and round in his mind.

He'd been flying every day: three or four sorties, weather permitting, for five days. The medical officer had been issuing Benzedrine tablets to keep them awake and alert.

Now he was the only man left of the original four to occupy the tent.

All the rest had bought it in one way or another – burnt, drowned, vaporized.

But they had decimated and unnerved two panzer divisions, though this had as yet made no impression on the battle in Normandy.

It was all so weirdly civilized. Every morning they sat in the mess, had bacon and eggs – if they could eat at all. Lately all he could manage was tea and toast, followed by a cigarette out in the sweet-smelling meadow.

Then came war, and death.

At night he was back in his bed, safe and cosy. It was surreal: more so than when he had been on Mosquitoes.

Then you didn't know quite so easily in the dark who wasn't making it back.

Here you sometimes saw them go down.

The morning briefing was as usual: the maximum effort would be against strong points and columns of enemy troops, especially armoured formations; they were to patrol at 15,000 feet and wait to be called in by ground controllers who had landed on D-Day +2 – like taxis from a rank.

Excitement, fear, violence, and tragedy: it was all going to happen again today, tomorrow, the day after. If there was a day after.

He wandered over to the mess post-rack; he had done so every day, but there was nothing for him.

He was turning away when the corporal sorting the letters into their pigeonholes held out a letter.

'One for you, sir.'

He took it, recognized her handwriting.

He didn't know whether to read it straight away, or leave it for later; they were due off in ten minutes.

Robbie made his mind up as he pulled on his Mae West, and opened it as he trudged out to his aircraft.

The fitter and airman waiting to help him into the cockpit and start the engine with the trolley ACK – a set of electrical batteries mounted on two car wheels that plugged into a point on the fuselage – watched as he suddenly stood rock still, reading the letter.

Puzzled, seconds passed before, to their amazement he suddenly yelled out:

'I'm going to be a father.'

With that he danced a little jig, then climbed up on to the wing, pumped the hand of the fitter and settled into the cockpit.

# CHAPTER THIRTY-EIGHT

John Fairfax was lying among the outbuildings of a farm. All day they had fought the German paratroopers, inching their way forward.

Now they were in the outskirts of Carentan, and it was a matter of house-to-house fighting, getting more desperate by the minute.

The Germans seemed almost suicidally brave, but there was a sense that their resistance was crumbling.

'One last push,' exhorted a major, leaping up. A hole appeared in his forehead and he pitched backwards with a surprised look on his face. His helmet rolled clear, exposing the back of his skull, which had burst apart, allowing his shattered brain to fall out.

John Fairfax, firing from the hip, took his place, leading a little group of dirty, dishevelled 'devils in baggy pants'. They cleared the building, but not before the two German paratroopers, fighting to the last, had been killed.

He led them out of the back into a yard with a waist-high stone wall. Crouching, he moved to its end, peered carefully around the corner.

Heavy machinegun fire made him jerk his head back. The stonework burst into fragments of masonry that rattled on his helmet and a cloud of dust shot into his eyes.

There was a roar and the sound of clanking, and tumbling bricks.

'Tanks.'

There was a deafening explosion and the building they'd just won disintegrated into a pile of rubble.

The tank rumbled forward as they fled, then flung themselves down into a ditch.

They watched as the Tiger tank in its distinctive dappled paint stopped; its turret track moved round, the aim of the barrel getting lower.

It fired.

Another explosion and the barn to their left, with half a dozen men in it, erupted into a great column of stone smithereens that rained down over the remains of the farm.

Firing erupted from all around as the panzer grenadiers who had been following the tank took up positions in their newly regained strongpoint.

From a point on rising ground Walter Raus followed the battle through his binoculars, standing on the seat of his Kubelwagon.

They had arrived in the nick of time. Now he watched and directed the action of the reconnaissance group, which was supported by five tanks, assault guns and flak wagons. The rest of the division was still some twenty kilometres away.

The Americans were lightly armed. For them the game was up. All his men had to do was drive the remainder of the paratroopers out, and then hold on till the main force could reach them.

After that they would go on the attack.

Smoke began to obstruct the view as the German guns opened up in a near continuous barrage.

Frowning, Walter waved his driver on.

'Get down to the crossroads.'

They'd taken up their 'taxi rank' position over the battlefield. Robbie had had only a few moments of thinking about the wonderful news contained in the letter in his top battledress pocket, when the R/T crackled.

They were directed to co-ordinates in the American section, to Carentan, where elements of a panzer group had stopped the advancing 101$^{st}$ Airborne Division.

Circling, they dropped down to 3000 feet, and soon the smoke of battle marked the area of fighting. The CO's voice came into his headphones.

'Target area is the centre of the farm and beyond. I'm going in to mark the aiming point. Red wing, deal with any flak, rest of you go for the tanks. Echelon port: all aircraft break left after attack and rejoin on the climb. Don't fire until you see that ahead is clear.'

With that he dropped a wing and dived down.

When it was his turn Robbie followed. The smoke was so thick that it was only when the scene was looming large in his windscreen that he could see a tank positioned on one side of a building.

He steadied the aiming point on the Tiger, then released two armour-piercing rockets. He watched the twin trails of the missiles converge on to the target. There was a huge eruption of flame and smoke, he saw a gun turret flying through the air, then he was climbing away.

Looking back he could see a stream of Typhoons still attacking.

He was halfway round when 88mm flak from a concealed wagon in a wood blasted into him. Instantly the cockpit went black with smoke and flames licked around his legs. There was only a second to bale out. He rolled the aircraft over, and tugged at the canopy.

It didn't budge.

The typhoon began to drop earthwards, its engine screaming in overload.

He tugged again – and again.

# CHAPTER THIRTY-NINE

The tanks didn't advance, just hunkered down in the ruins, blasting away with their main armament and sweeping the area with machinegun fire.

John Fairfax heard the signals officer giving out co-ordinates from a map held on his thigh, calling for air support or naval gunfire. Under the covering fire the German infantry was beginning to work round them; the bloody 'cavalry' had better get to them soon.

Suddenly somebody yelled:

'Grenade.'

At the same moment he saw the dark shape of the 'potato-masher' fall out of the sky and land beside him. He scrabbled it away with his feet, just as it exploded with a searing heat and a blast of shrapnel.

Violent pain knifed into his body and legs, and a moment of incredible light lit up his existence, then everything went black.

Walter Raus leapt out of his Scout car and ran for the cover of a concrete walled pigsty, his radio man with him.

In minutes he'd assessed the situation. They had achieved their goal. Now all that was needed was for the rest of the column to get here on time.

'Sir.'

A young Schultz ran up and saluted, hollow sunken eyes under his steel helmet stared white out of a dark, oil-streaked face.

'Yes?'

'We have prisoners, sir. What shall we do?'

Walter Raus grimaced at the inexperience of his young warriors. Nobody would have asked him that on the Ost Front.

'Bring them out and get them back to Intelligence.'

'Sir.'

Two minutes later seven Americans without helmets, four with their hands on the tops of their heads, trailed past under guard. The last one was on a makeshift stretcher, carried by the other two. He had a blood soaked bandage round his head and chest, his trousers were ripped open revealing further filthy rags tied around the white flesh beneath.

Walter Raus could see that he was an officer. He called for the column to halt and crossed to him.

'You are a leutnant?'

Guardedly, through his blurred vision and pain, John Fairfax nodded.

'Yeah.'

Walter took out a cigarette, lit it, and passed it to him.

Amazed, John Fairfax put it to his trembling lips as the German said: 'Come with me. We will get you to a field dressing-station in my car.'

His makeshift stretcher was lifted on to the back of a Kubelwagon. They began bumping and grinding along a road, every jolt causing him to grit his teeth with the pain.

Only minutes had elapsed before the dreaded roar of aircraft was heard. Immediately the wagon turned sharply in under some trees. Leaping out, Walter ordered his prisoner to be lifted off and put into a ditch.

They were near to two flak wagons, which began a deafening barrage as the roar started to turn to whines.

Lying flat, Walter didn't need to use binoculars to watch the RAF planes – those hated Typhoons – wreak havoc on his tanks. Great columns of oily black smoke marked the death of each one. It was all over in less than fifteen minutes.

And in that moment he realized that there was no hope of the main column getting through – not in daylight. And in any case, when they did, the overwhelming air superiority of the Allies had spelt the end for tanks in this war – probably even, for ever,

Then suddenly there was cheering as one of the Typhoons flew straight into the angry red-and-black puffs of ack-ack.

Immediately it shuddered, pulled up, flames streaking down its length.

The cheers were short-lived as the howl of an aero engine drowned out everything. Walter slammed into the dirt alongside his prisoner anticipating the blast of rockets, or the chewing-up of ground and flesh by cannon fire.

In the event it was rockets. The ground jumped up and smacked into John Fairfax's body, causing him to scream out in agony.

Walter Raus was thrown several feet as the explosions blew a flak wagon to pieces.

Seconds later two more detonations tore up the earth, turning the second flak wagon into a burning wreck.

Screaming, groaning and desperate shouts came from all around.

Walter Raus, coughing, his mouth full of dirt, his cap gone, got to his knees, then staggered up. The scene of carnage was horrendous.

He came across a crater with a piece of the flak wagon still burning. Around it were the dismembered bodies of the crew, most stripped of their uniforms, while some thirty feet away a very young fresh-faced youth, dead, blond hair shining in the light, was unmarked.

How strange the ways of death.

Further on were more bodies, and the crack and flare of exploding shells.

Shocked and trembling he made his way back to the scout car. If he hadn't known it before the Russian front, he certainly knew it now. There was a terrible folly in this vast conflict that had caused so much suffering. War was obscene.

They picked up the groaning American and put him back on the Kubelwagon. Walter barked an order at the green-looking driver to get behind the wheel. As the man gunned the engine he took a last look back at Carentan. He could see American paratroopers dodging from cover to cover as they swarmed into the town, where the grenadiers were falling back, running, sometimes dropping.

He turned away.

His eyes constantly searched the sky as they continued down the road.

As they approached yet another burning wreck, a half-track, with bodies and craters all around it, the driver had to brake and swerve to avoid a figure, a figure in the torn but still recognizable uniform of a panzer grenadier, covered in blood and dirt.

Walter raised his arm, snapped at his driver.

'Stop.'

He swung his legs out and walked back. He looked at the figure and recoiled in horror.

The man had no face, just raw white bone sticking out of torn flesh;

the eye sockets were empty, there were no ears, one hand was gone.

It was not possible that such a thing could live – or would want to live.

The figure continued staggering around until it tripped and fell to the ground screaming in agony.

Walter Raus took out his Luger from its holster, worked a shell into the chamber, and walked over to the pitiable creature.

In the panzer divisions, they always told new recruits that you had only fifteen seconds to get out of a burning tank, and therefore they should always have their gun ready. It was better to die cleanly by your own hand than to exist for another minute and be burned to death.

And that was what was required here – though the man could not do it himself.

He raised his arm, and fired two rounds, – one into the hideous face, and the other into the heart.

Despite his agony John Fairfax had seen everything, but all Water Raus said when he came back was:

'It was for the better.'

By nightfall, with the thunder of the huge naval guns rumbling far inland, rolling and echoing across the fields and through the villages, the flashes flickering like lightning across the dark sky, Walter Raus, exhausted, leaned back on the wing of the Kubelwagon, smoking a cheroot.

He knew by then, that the end of the war, defeat, had just come a little closer.

The success of the Allied landing was now not in doubt.

The Second Front was a reality.

Oh, they might be able to secure defensive positions along the River Orne or the Seine, but it would only be a matter of time.

Rommel had been right, and thanks to Hitler's prevarication and stubbornness, their moment had passed.

Allied air power, he knew, would spell the end of the Wehrmacht in the West. The fighter bombers coming in just above tree height with their heart-stopping scream of aero engines had paralysed all daylight movement.

The roads were becoming blocked with burning panzers, trucks, and the bodies of men and horses. Everywhere, in lanes and fields were the bloated, putrefying bodies of hundreds of cows. The stench of death hung in the air. The Allies had learnt well the lesson of the blitzkrieg of 1940.

Against it, the Germans' much-vaunted panzers were powerless.

He thought of the end of the Third Reich.

Above all, he thought of Inge.

# CHAPTER FORTY

Maddie was with Mrs Kaplinsky when it happened.

She had to stop playing as the noise of the motorbike outside in the street grew louder and louder. The heavily accented voice of her tutor exclaimed:

'Oh really, vill those army people please go away.'

Then it stopped – completely. There was absolute silence.

'Right.' Mrs Kaplinsky tapped her fan on the piano. 'Resume from the top of the page.'

Maddie began again. She'd barely played four bars of a Beethoven sonata when an immense explosion rocked the building. Screaming, the two women were thrown to the floor as all the windows blew in and the curtains ripped wildly in the blast. Lumps of the ceiling came down, smashing rows of porcelain figurines, and hitting the piano with such force that one leg buckled. The piano keeled over and slammed to the floor with a terrific crash. A thick fog of plaster dust filled the room.

Eventually, wild-eyed and covered in white plaster, eyes big and red-rimmed, Maddie got to the older woman.

'Mrs Kaplinsky, are you all right?'

The prone figure moaned. Gently Maddie turned her over. From a gash over her left eye a rivulet of red blood stood out starkly against the white powder.

Both women's hair was standing on end.

'Are you all right?' Maddie repeated.

Mrs Kaplinsky's eyes opened, blinked.

'Vot vos that, vot happened?'

'I don't know.'

Outside they could hear the bells of emergency vehicles – and people screaming.

She got Mrs Kaplinsky propped against the still humming piano before she went to the glassless window and carefully leaned out.

The street was a mass of rubble and scattered broken chimney pots. Gates lay at crazy angles.

Down the road and across on the other side, there was a huge gap in the terrace, as though a tooth had been ripped from a row of teeth. Two houses were completely gone. And, more sickening, there were torn limbs lying in the street and embedded in hedges. The gutters were running with blood.

Maddie convulsed and vomit spewed from her mouth, so badly that she was worried for the safety of the baby.

When it stopped she went back to Mrs Kaplinsky. What she found frightened her. The old lady had lapsed into unconsciousness.

Maddie ran out into the street to get help from the firemen and ambulance men who were covering the dead and collecting the body parts.

Two men came back with her. When they'd taken Mrs Kaplinsky away Maddie didn't know what do to; she ended up aimlessly wandering about, doing her best to comfort survivors.

She found another old lady clutching a dead Pekinese to her chest. Maddie eventually managed to get her to part with the little body and got the woman into a neighbour's house which had been turned into a casualty clearing-station.

She didn't know how it had happened – how it was that she had been missed, but she stumbled on to a little girl of six or seven, lying, with her bicycle in the gutter of a lane, sightless blue eyes staring into an equally blue sky.

She collapsed.

They kept her in overnight for observation. She had had traces of blood on her underclothes, and there was a fear that she had begun to abort. In the end they reassured her that, for the moment at least, the baby was safe.

She enquired after Mrs Kaplinsky but they seemed to be guarded about saying anything about her: she wasn't a relative, was she?

Just before Maddie left in the ambulance that was taking her and several other women back to their homes, she overheard a staff nurse speaking to two men dressed in sombre dark clothes in the main entrance.

'Yes, that's right. Mrs Kaplinsky will be having a Jewish funeral.'

Shocked, Maddie sat in the ambulance, numb, as the driver and his mate talked non-stop about Hitler's revenge weapons the papers had been reporting on recently. Had that explosion been one of them? There had been mystery explosions in Kent and Sussex, and one in Bethnal Green on 13 June. She thought she'd scream if the ambulancemen didn't shut up.

At last she was standing on the corner of her street. Despite the warmth, she wrapped her coat tightly around her, feeling wretched. If only Robbie was with her. She ached to have his arms around her. There had been no letter or phone calls for nearly three weeks now.

Later, doing her shopping, queueing for her butter and sugar ration the terrible droning noise came again, like a motorbike in the heavens. Terrified, she sheltered in a shop doorway and searched the sky as people started running in all directions.

The guns in the parks thundered but could not erase that awful throbbing noise. Suddenly people pointed – and she saw it, a dark cylindrical-shape with stubby wings and a red pulsating flame at the rear, flying serenely through all the black puffs of exploding shells.

It droned past, and was only a speck in the darkening sky when the noise abruptly stopped.

Maddie remembered that awful silence from before, and ran deeper into the shop, crouched down, hands to her ears, eyes tightly shut, with her back to the street.

The explosion, though some distance away was thunderous, echoing down the streets. Maddie could hardly contain her trembling.

She wanted Robbie so much. Maybe it was because of the baby inside her, but she felt so vulnerable – and alone.

# CHAPTER FORTY-ONE

For Sally the days turned into a week, then another, and still there was no word from him. Weeks in which Hitler's secret weapon, pilotless flying bombs, began to rain down on Southern England.

Already there had been 2,500 deaths and 8,000 injured. This new onslaught was testing everybody severely, as there had been an expectation that the war might be over by Christmas.

Thanks to her worry over John, she'd only nearly missed being a casualty herself. One had fallen on the Guards Chapel within half a mile of Downing Street, killing 200 senior officers and civil servants who had assembled to give thanks for the successful D-Day landings.

Sally had been invited, but had declined. She didn't know how she managed to keep working, keep concentrating, but she did. It was what they all had done, were still doing.

She was at her desk when the American major appeared before her. She could see in his eyes that something had happened, that he had something to tell her.

Her heart rate doubled as she stood up, then held on to the desk as her legs started to buckle.

'Oh God, is it bad. Is he. . . ?'

He took her by the arm, and said quickly:

'No, no, its OK. He's in hospital, here in England.'

Sally was frightened.

'Hospital?'

'Yes, he's got leg and back injuries, but he's not going to die.'

The word die was like a cold knife thrust into her belly, making her imagination run wild.

When she eventually got her breath back she said:

'I must go to him now.'

The major shuffled his feet uncomfortably.

'They don't allow visitors, Sally; they ship them back home – Stateside – as soon as possible.'

She shook her head adamantly.

'No – no. I must get to him.'

He tried to say it was impossible, but she would have none of it.

In the end he went away, saying he would see what he could do.

It was late evening when he got back to her. She was still on duty, saw him coming across the busy room.

He grinned nervously.

'You'll get me court-martialled. Here, I've got an order for you to take a signal to him – urgently. With SHAEF's stamp on it you're not going to get any trouble.' He pushed an envelope into her hands.

Sally, uniformed, on duty or not, went up on her toes and kissed him quickly on the cheek.

'Al – you're a pal. I won't forget this.' Then she made for the door.

He called after her.

'Take something official-looking to carry it in.'

Next day, in uniform and grasping her rail warrant, she set off with a leather bag on her hip, its strap across her chest and shoulder. It was the one in which she kept her notebooks. She'd added a few meaningless documents for extra effect.

The journey was long, with delays and poor connections as the overloaded railways in southern England tried to cope with the huge traffic of troops and supplies bound for the ports – and France.

On a platform, as the air-raid sirens sounded yet again, she wondered what she was going to see, what awful maiming might he have suffered?

In the waiting-room into which they were shepherded, she found a spot to sit, and began to dash off a note to leave with him. She couldn't trust herself to say all the things she wanted to, and in any case she didn't know how long she would be allowed to stay, or whether, in fact, he would be conscious at all.

That frightened her.

She wanted John to know that whatever had happened to him – to his body – it didn't matter.

All she wanted was to be with him.

# CHAPTER FORTY-TWO

For days now they had been bombarded by artillery, and wave after wave of bombers.

When the latest formation had rumbled into the distance, an exhausted Walter Raus lifted his head above the edge of the slit trench he was in, and looked out at the surreal world all around him.

They were in a cemetery, or rather the remains of one. Dust from the bombing hung thickly in the air. As it slowly cleared, shapes loomed out of the fog.

Stone crosses lay at crazy angles, and 'angels' stood without heads or wings.

Worst of all some of the bodies had been lifted from their 'last' resting place, resurrected into the nightmare that was the battle for Caen, their winding sheets flapping in the breeze.

Swarms of flies were everywhere. He slapped his face as they tried to settle on him.

British tanks were massing for another attack, and this time Walter knew they would break through.

He had no radio communication with any of his units, and had sent off a runner to try and find out what was happening. Almost as soon as he'd gone, another figure covered in dust rolled into the trench.

The helmetless unterscharführer crouched down beside him.

'Sir, can you tell me what's going on? I'm out of touch with my platoon.'

Walter shook his head, but before he could reply they heard the clanking and roar of tanks.

The British came out of the village ruins ahead, charging straight at them, the caterpillar tracks churning up earth, causing some of the bodies to 'sit up' before collapsing back into the dust.

Walter had nothing left to fight with but his Luger.

One of the tanks made straight for them, loomed ever larger. Ineffectually he tried shooting at the driver's hatch until at the last moment they had to fling themselves into the bottom of the trench.

The Sherman went right over them. In the split second of roaring, diesel-smelling blackness he knew the time had come. There was still a round in the chamber and another in the magazine. On the Ost Front they had sworn an oath never to be taken alive, but did that apply here in the West?

He thought of Inge and their unborn child. Could he leave them by his own hand?

Then the heavy caterpillar tracks began to collapse the walls, burying them in earth as the tank moved on.

He lost his grip on the Luger; his hands moved in panic to scrabble at the soil packing into his mouth and nose.

Suddenly hands seized him by the arms and dragged him out into bright daylight.

Two British Tommies held him on either side.

One said:

'Got a bloody SS officer, like a rat in a hole.'

Another voice growled: 'Put your fuckin' hands on your head Fritz.'

He did as he was told, stumbling and dazed as rifle butts drove him into captivity.

But all he could think of was the knowledge that he would have broken his vow.

Inge and the unborn child meant more to him than anything else in the world.

More than being in the SS.

More even, than the Fatherland.

# CHAPTER FORTY-THREE

His visitor came in the evening.

John Fairfax couldn't quite make out who it was because of the strong, low sunshine coming through a window in the corridor behind. When the figure came closer he could see it was an Army padre.

At first he thought he was just on a routine visit, then his eyes fell on Sally's torn and dusty bag in the man's hands, the one in which she kept her notebooks, and he knew that something was terribly wrong.

He listened in stunned, disbelieving silence. The padre didn't tell him all the details – didn't know them himself, like how the V1 had fallen silently out of the sky. She'd not died instantly, but had managed to push her bag into the hands of a rescue worker as the man had leant down over her, trying to free her from the iron girder that had crushed her chest. Blood had trickled from her mouth, her face and hair had been caked in dust.

The priest gently told him only that before she had died she'd whispered, 'Tell him I'm sorry.' That was all.

Even he did not know that the rescue worker had watched as the colour drained out of her green eyes, and the pupils had enlarged, becoming dark and lifeless.

The rescuer had called out:

'This one's gone. Give me a canvas sheet.'

They had to sedate John Fairfax, frightened that he would open his wounds as he thrashed around in his own hell.

Days later, as he was being carefully hoisted off the dockside and lowered on to the deck of the boat taking him home, he'd heard, then seen one of the German flying bombs, already called doodlebugs by the English. As its harsh throbbing caused thousands on the quayside to look upwards fearfully, he'd felt hate for the first time in his war.

Everybody waited with bated breath for the motor to cut out, but it kept droning on until it was out of sight.

They were coming over at the rate of 100 a day, a medic had said, and they had killed thousands.

And one of them had been her.

As the west coast of Ireland, and with it Europe, receded into the distance at the end of the white wake left by the hospital ship, he stared blankly down the length of his shattered body, and the battered bag that he refused to let go of.

Shattered body, shattered dreams.

There was nothing left inside him.

# CHAPTER FORTY-FOUR

Walter Raus was stripped of his Knights Cross, kept in an officers' compound with a hundred others. They would stand in a snaking line in the rain for food dispensed by cooks from converted oil drums. Heavily armed guards looked on.

There was a humiliating feeling of helplessness, of being cut off from the world. A prisoner had no news, had nothing to do but look out from behind the wire at the dreary muddy battle-torn landscape.

Then one day four British military police in their distinctive red caps, led by an officer, came and escorted him out of the compound into the office of the camp commandant.

The man looked up at him as he stood before his desk and said without preamble.

'You are being transferred to a prison in England. There you will be charged with war crimes, mainly the shooting in cold blood of a RAF prisoner of war who had been shot down while attacking your armoured column shortly after D-Day. There are other charges relating to your time on the Eastern front as a member of the Waffen SS.'

Walter was shocked, and started to protest his innocence. The man took no notice, made no reply, just nodded.

Walter's hands were pulled behind his back, and handcuffs were roughly clamped around his wrists.

Still in shock, he was led out in front of all the other prisoners and put into a car, with two huge 'Redcaps' as the British military police were called, on either side of him on the back seat.

He was aware of many of the ordinary Wehrmacht officers turning their backs on him. They drove off to an airfield.

During the flight in a twin-engined transport that he heard referred to as a Dakota, and as he stepped for the first time on damp English soil, he could only think of Inge, and the grief and shame he was bringing on her.

He wished he had kept his oath and put a bullet through his brain.

# CHAPTER FORTY-FIVE

Maddie was at her piano, lost in Chopin's Nocturne Op 9 No 2, before a packed audience in an East End hall.

There was a moment's silence when she finished, then the applause came in a rush.

She stood, one hand on the piano and took a bow.

And another.

It was then that she noticed two air force officers at the back of the hall, at the entrance. One of them was a padre. They looked grave. The men on door duty pointed to her.

She knew then, knew with utter certainty that Robbie had left her, that she would not see him again in this life.

Not a sound passed her lips, she was as silent as the grave. Yet she screamed, screamed, and was still screaming as they led her to a side room, mouthing words she couldn't hear. Something about missing in action. . . .

Somebody took her home, made tea.

She lay on her bed, knew that several people were in her kitchen, whispering.

The passing of days, then weeks, led to no further news.

Robbie was finally posted: 'Killed in Action'.

He had disappeared off the face of the earth, seemingly never to be heard of again.

Maddie would have ended it all then and there; she wanted to be with him, there was no more point to her existence.

She felt no guilt, as a Catholic, about taking her life, but inside her was a living, growing, testament to their union.

It was Robbie's child, his future. There was no way she could destroy that.

Maddie gave up her studies; she could not carry on, her heart was dead.

They were very good to her. Sir Miles interceded with the board, telling them that he had found her of remarkable promise – a promise that had only become evident in the last few months.

Other staff agreed, and Maddie was offered a bursary for the following year, to complete her course, once she had had the baby.

Her depression, her feeling of utter desolation only lifted with the first cramping pain of the onset of labour.

She was back in Ireland, with the Sisters of Charity. As she had expected, as an unmarried mother she was not welcome at home. Her father had threatened to lock her out rather than bring shame on the family.

The baby girl was born at 5.45, at sunrise, and was named Bridie by the nuns, after the delivery sister.

She was immediately taken from Maddie and placed in the weaning room, and a family who had already given a donation were informed that their baby was ready for adoption.

Maddie, as soon as she realized what was happening, got out of bed, nearly falling to the floor because her legs were so weak.

Unseen, she managed to dress. She tiptoed to the weaning room and instantly recognized her baby with her shock of black hair and blue eyes.

When the nun in charge was away she rushed in and picked the infant up. The bracelet on her wrist said 'Bridie O'Connor'.

Maddie grabbed a blanket and wrapped her in it.

The walk in the drizzle down the gravel drive to the big iron gates on the main road seemed to go on for ever. She tensed, expecting shouts, but none ever came.

As she waited for a bus she sheltered in a shop doorway and gave the baby her first little feed.

Maddie took only her purse and the English money she had hidden in the lining of her coat.

Later, on the boat as she watched the coast of Ireland disappear into the rain-swept distance she threw the name band with 'Bridie O'Connor' on it into the sea, and looked at the little face buried in the blanket in the crook of her arm, and whispered:

'Dawn – I'll call you Dawn. You were born at dawn and this will be a new dawn for all of us.'

# CHAPTER FORTY-SIX

John Fairfax was shipped straight to the Walter Reed Hospital in Washington DC.

Throughout the next few months he underwent several operations on his back. They also had to remove a tiny piece of fragmented bone lying on the surface of his brain.

Of his war he could now remember very little, only of being dropped on D-Day with nearly 20,000 British, Canadian and American Paratroopers, who had started out with such hope in their hearts and fear in their bellies.

After the battle for Carentan, and his capture, he had only a vague memory of diving planes, and a terrible paralysing roar; then nothing till he had come out of a fever to find a doctor bending over him, a military doctor; holding a lamp. Or was it someone else?

The doctor had said:

*'Es steht schlecht um ihn.'*

Suddenly there had been a tremendous explosion followed closely by another, and rubble and dust had poured down on him, his last recollection before he'd blacked out again.

The next time he came to it had been quite peaceful, and there were other men in the room, a row of them in beds like himself.

It hadn't been until a nurse, an American Army nurse, had come over to him that he'd realized it was a hospital, in England.

And then had come the dreadful, heart-stopping news.

It was only later, much later, that he understood he owed his life, in the first instance to the German officer who had got him to a first-aid post so quickly, where he received initial medical treatment, and then to the arrival of General Omar Bradley's First Army, and with them a new drug called penicillin.

He'd known nothing of the shelling, the bombing, the screaming, the dreadful frightening silence, then the sound of running boots, the crack of carbines and staccato bursts of machinegun fire. Eventually the double doors of the once grand room were kicked open and American troops broke in with guns aimed at them.

He'd been unaware of the amputee's greeting, from the next bed to the men of the 4th Infantry Division with the welcoming: 'What took you so fuckin' long?'

He'd been evacuated back to England through Cherbourg, the letter 'M' written on his forehead to show that he'd been given morphine, as well as the penicillin in his butt, and powder on the open wounds of his chest and back.

All for what? After Sally's death he just didn't want to live, and he was tormented by the sight he had seen from his stretcher of the hundreds of body bags on the wharf at Cherbourg. Even in a so-called noble cause, was it ever worth it? Certainly not for those eighteen- and nineteen-year-olds or their loved ones.

At long last they declared he was fit to travel home to Maine.

During his time in hospital he had received visits from his father and mother, and even Sis. They were worried, not only about his physical injuries, which they were told would leave him requiring a wheelchair, but by his mental state.

He was so withdrawn, so listless, so different from the boy who had gone off to war.

The psychiatrists had tried to help, but knew nothing of her; he couldn't bring himself to talk about Sally's death to anyone, because she was still there, inside him. If he said anything aloud to other people, he knew she would somehow be released, like a bird, and fly away.

And he didn't want her to go.

Just before they arrived to take him home, as he was packing, he found himself holding her battered leather bag. He'd never been able to open it, until now.

With her notebooks there was a letter, addressed to him. He looked at the envelope for ages before he could bring himself to open it.

There was just the one scented sheet.

She said she loved him, and whatever his injuries, he was not to worry, that all she wanted was him, nothing else.

And when they were eventually married, she would never let him be as much as one night away from her ever again. He was her kindred spirit.

It was then that he realized he was never again going to look into those lovely green eyes, look right into her soul, or she into his.

He began to cry, like a baby.

# CHAPTER FORTY-SEVEN

Inge eventually received a message through the Red Cross that Walter was a prisoner. There was no mention of the charges he faced. She was overjoyed, in that he was at least safe: no longer in danger. She was trying to write back when the pain started.

In the dimly lit hospital cellar Inge gave birth during an RAF raid. The little boy lasted twenty minutes, but died as the sirens sounded the all-clear.

A week later she resumed her duties, but now she rarely smiled; she became more withdrawn.

At the end of March, terror started to take hold in the city when it became clear that the Anglo-Americans would not be coming.

Tales of horrors meted out to the civilian population in East Prussia at the hands of the Asiatic hordes of the Red Army, particularly the rape of women, spread like wildfire.

The railway stations and bus terminals were becoming jammed with women and children fleeing west.

On 12 April Inge went to the last concert of the Berlin Philharmonic. It ended with the finale of Wagner's *Götterdämerung*.

Then one morning the bombardment commenced.

Although it was many kilometres away across the city, the whole building shook and quivered, jugs of water wobbled on bedside tables, and charts and pictures dropped to the floor.

Telephones rang and groups of nurses and patients stood in huddled fearful groups.

It was the start of the Russian attack on the capital.

Not long afterwards the hospital, along with most others, was evacuated to a large stone-built barracks.

Through all the horror of what followed, Inge worked on. Then the bitter fighting started in their district. Terrified patients and staff lay under the beds as bullets, grenades and point-blank artillery rounds were fired just outside.

When eventually the front-line troops of the victorious Red Army broke into the hospital, they raced through the wards searching for Nazis, but left the nurses alone.

But the soldiers who came next were different, and when the capitulation came, and with it the euphoria at having survived the bloodiest war in history, the trouble started.

The soldiers drank all the alcohol stocks in the hospital, and even started on chemicals from the laboratories.

The first one to rape Inge was a Russian officer who put the barrel of his pistol into her mouth and held it there throughout the attack which took place in the middle of the ward.

Others followed, and soon she, like all the women, feared the 'hunting hours' after an evening of drinking.

Because Berlin was in ruins, the screams of women could be heard in the night down all the streets.

But she survived, detaching her mind from her body, thinking of all the wonderful times that had gone before.

And of Walter.

And that some time they would be together again.

# CHAPTER FORTY-EIGHT

Maddie was back in London when the war in Europe came to an end. She had changed her name to Cochran.

As she finished work at a bus terminal canteen – she wasn't due to start back at the academy until October – drivers and clippies were suddenly shouting the news and sounding the horns of the buses in the garage.

On the way home she was caught up in the crowds thronging central London, cheering, singing, kissing.

She was grabbed several times and didn't try to stop the young servicemen from all over the world celebrating the fact that they were going, after all, to live, to enjoy full, long lives.

They deserved it.

But her heart wasn't in it. She and Robbie had been denied that. When at last she got back to her digs it was to find her landlady, Mrs Adams, had baby Dawn nestling in her arm in a Welsh shawl, a glass of stout in the other hand.

'Isn't it wonderful?'

Knowing that Mrs Adams's husband was in the Eighth Army somewhere, she did her best to be jolly, but the effort as she joined in with the neighbours, playing the upright piano in the front room as they all gathered around lustily singing 'There'll Always Be An England', 'Roll Out the Barrel', and all the old favourites that had kept them going in the dark days of defeat and tragedy, in the end left her drained.

She put Dawn to bed at eight o'clock, but the little girl was overtired, and didn't really go to sleep until ten.

Left alone in the house, as Mrs Adams had gone to the corner pub, which was reportedly going to stay open all night – or at least until the beer ran out, she settled once more at the piano.

Her eyes were moist as she said softly: 'This is for you my darling.'

Greig's Piano Concerto rang out as outside, crowds continued dancing and singing in the newly lit streets.

# CHAPTER FORTY-NINE

John Fairfax persuaded his father to put off taking him to his Rotary Club, to show off his Silver Star and Purple Heart; he'd been awarded the Star for his leadership and the bayonet charge at the end of the Causeway.

He felt – knew – his actions had not been special. Over the entire disastrous drop zone on that murderous, confused night, the battle had been won by small groups of troopers from many units getting together, making a difference.

His action had not been something special, many had died doing the same thing; others, before they had had a chance to show what they had got, drowned in the areas the enemy had flooded, or had been shot as they had swung helplessly in their harness. No, he could not bring himself to be wheeled in as someone special. He had learned of the dignity and nobility of the common man.

The day came when he felt strong enough to do what he had been longing to do since the day he'd come home: take the dogs to the beach – on his own.

They drove him to the boardwalk that led down to the sand. It took a lot, especially for his mother, to leave him there as he wheeled himself down to the beach.

For her, one of her worst fears had been realized. She had said goodbye to a fit young son, and he had come home a cripple.

It had taken all her strength to carry on as normal in front of him. But his father had had to comfort her during many a night in the privacy of their bedroom.

The dogs were gone in a flash, wagging tails, disappearing through what was left of a picket fence now half-submerged by a sand dune.

He could hear them barking as they raced along the water's edge.

He kneaded his aching thighs where the bullets had smashed the bone, before pulling a packet of Camels out of his top pocket and lighting up.

So it was all, finally, over. Roosevelt and Hitler were dead, Hirohito a mere mortal, Churchill was gone from power, Truman was now the President, and nothing ever would be the same again. Only Uncle Joe Stalin remained.

He felt the salt-laden breeze on his face, closed his eyes and listened to the ocean.

It could have been in Cornwall.

A lump came into his throat as he recalled how she had looked that first time, striding along the beach.

It was that then he remembered Sally's notebooks: wondered. . . .

The idea grew, and with it the conviction that somehow she would be guiding his hand as he wrote the book she had been so cruelly prevented from doing. He remembered the title she had teased him with . . . *Softly Falls the Moonlight*.

He suddenly had a burning desire to immerse himself in the past, to be with her again, as he drew their story from the notes she had left.

But later, when he was home, as he was wheeled into the hall, the phone rang. His mother took it as his father positioned him near the big window in the family room, ready for lunch.

His mother came in, looked excited – and hesitant at the same time.

'It's Betty. That was her father. She's coming home today – they want us to go round tomorrow evening.'

John Fairfax looked uncomfortable.

'I'm not sure she'll be that keen to see me, Mom,' he shrugged, 'like this.'

'I see.'

His mother had guessed all along.

'That's not it. You've ended it with her, haven't you?'

He'd ducked a direct answer.

'Sort of, said we ought to back off while the world was still burning.'

Actually, he'd written,

*People change, Betty, and I am no longer the boy you knew. Please don't think the worst of me but I think it would be wise if we realize that what we had is in the past. Please, wherever you are, look to the future.*

His mother had raised an eyebrow, in the way only his mother could.

'Whilst the world is still burning? How poetical of you John, but I think it's our duty to go, don't you?'

When his mother spoke like that, he knew it was no good protesting.

It was only a short drive to Betty's house. The front door opened without their having to press the bell. The parents warmly exchanged handshakes and hugs with each other, then her mother and father leaned down to do the same to him.

'How's our hero then?' asked Betty's father.

He winced, said something inane as her mother fussed over him, arranging the blanket over his legs. The evenings were getting chilly.

Drinks were served. He asked for a beer. There was still no sign of Betty as he finished it, and was served another.

At last, in answer to their unspoken question, her mother looked anxiously at them all.

'She'll be down in a minute, she's exhausted.'

She faced his mother.

'Betty tires very easily, Eleanor; you'll see a change in her.'

Her father shot a nervous glance at the staircase, before turning to him.

'She's been through a lot. A kamikaze hit her hospital ship off Okinawa. They made it under destroyer escort into the harbour at Guam, but she lost a lot of friends. It's affected her.'

Her mother fiddled nervously with her handkerchief. 'Like you John, we're lucky to have her back. We thank God every night. She's had dengue fever and malaria, I nearly died when I first saw her.'

Eventually a lavatory flushed and there was the sound of footsteps at the top of the stairs.

Her legs showed first. There was no flesh, only bones and skin. When the rest of her came into view he was appalled.

She had lost so much weight that her previously tailored skirt hung loosely, revealing hardly any curves to her figure. Her neck and arms showed the ropy muscles beneath her yellowing skin.

As she reached the bottom and came into the room, he swallowed hard. Betty had always had lovely, thick, luxurious hair. He used to joke with her about the number of times she washed its shiny blonde waves.

Now it was short and lacklustre. Her face was pinched and sallow.

She said hello to his parents first, before she stood over him.

There had been one more change.

She stooped down held out her hand and said:

'Hi John.' He looked into her eyes. They had always been carefree, showing nothing but the innocence and hope in her soul.

Now, they had a steely quality and, paradoxically a vulnerability; they were eyes that had seen terrible things; windows to a soul that was no longer innocent in the ways of mankind.

'Hi Betty.'

She gave a humourless smile, leaned nearer and whispered:

'Is this enough change for you?'

Shamed, he stuttered: 'Betty, I'm – I'm sorry, I didn't mean to hurt you.'

She touched his arm reassuringly, the gesture having a professional feel. Then he remembered she'd been – was – a nurse. Soothingly she whispered:

'There's no need John, no need at all.' Then she'd straightened up and turned to the others.

For the next half-hour the conversation slowly improved, at least for the parents, with the occasional involvement of Betty and John. They did not engage in any direct talk.

That didn't come until they were out on the back porch, looking at a wonderfully clear Maine night sky, the stars hard and twinkling like diamonds against a velvet background. The darkness made it easier to talk. She took out her cigarettes, offered him one from the pack.

He took it, accepted a light. The flame illuminated his face which, unobserved by him, she looked at intently.

When he pulled back and breathed out the first lungful of smoke he said:

'That's a nice lighter.'

It had been a man's, made of gunmetal.

'Belonged to a good friend of mine.'

He'd seen the medical corps insignia on it. She didn't say any more.

So there had been a tragedy in her life as well.

In a strange way it had made him feel better. She lit her cigarette; her hands, he noticed, were slightly trembling.

'How you really doing, Betty?' he'd asked.

She chuckled.

'Never felt better – and you?'

He smiled, really smiled, slapped the side of the wheelchair.

'Me too. Never felt better.'

A bond formed. They'd been where others had never trod, would never understand. They sat, saying nothing, just smoking, looking at the heavens, the better side of God's creation.

Eventually he said:

'A nurse, eh? Never knew you wanted that, Betty.'

The end of her cigarette had glowed for a second before she'd replied.

'There were a lot of things I never knew I wanted, until war came along.'

He knew what she meant.

After a while he asked: 'You going to carry on nursing?'

In the darkness, unseen, she'd shaken her head.

'Can't for a bit, not with what I've picked up. Later, who knows? God has a way of taking things into his own hands when mere mortals start thinking they can control their world.'

He regarded the Milky Way above.

'Do you still believe in him?'

He had to wait a few moments for her reply, after she had taken a last pull on her cigarette.

'If I hadn't, I'd have lost my mind, it's as simple as that, but now – when there's time to reflect, to think . . .' She left it unanswered, stubbed out the cigarette, stood up.

'Shall we get back inside? I'm feeling pretty tired.'

With difficulty he insisted on opening the screen door into the back lobby, and paused.

'May I see you again?'

She looked at him uneasily, started to say, 'I don't think—' but he quickly interrupted with: 'Betty, not like that, but I've enjoyed tonight very much. Perhaps we could share a cup of coffee one morning, just get back to feeling normal, not like some endangered species in a zoo? It helps to have something in common.'

She took her time, before she eventually nodded.

'Yes, I'd like that. I'll call you.'

# CHAPTER FIFTY

Walter Raus stood ramrod straight as the charges were read out.

To each one – he spoke excellent English and had declined the services of an interpreter – he answered with an emphatic 'Not Guilty.'

It was a relatively short trial, just two days in total.

He sat bolt upright in his chair in the dock, flanked by two British military policemen, and showed no emotion as the case against him was outlined, and witnesses presented, who said they had definitely seen him shoot an RAF pilot who had been captured after baling out.

The accused had been in command of a panzer SS unit that had just been strafed by the prisoner.

Through their binoculars, two artillery forward observers had seen the whole incident.

Later, accusations were submitted in writing from a Russian political officer attached to a guards regiment. SS Sturmbannführer Walter Raus had ordered the machinegunning of 300 prisoners of war near the town of Bryansk in the summer of 1943.

The captain appointed to lead his defence was struggling, Walter could see that.

He had attempted to show that at the time of the incident with the RAF pilot, Walter was a couple of kilometres away, in a different sector.

Despite extensive enquiries, not a single surviving member of his regiment had been with him that day.

An American officer of whom Walter had spoken could not be traced in time for the trial, but efforts were still being made in America.

The court was not indulgent. Several months had already passed without result; adjournments could not be open-ended commitments.

The captain, however, made short work of the Russian accusation. From unit and formation records it was obvious that he had never been nearer than one hundred kilometres from the massacre at the time stated, and a German security battalion had been engaged in a scorched-earth exercise in the area.

When he was asked to speak, Walter was concise, and unemotional; too much so for his own good, thought the captain.

When the time came Walter stood as the verdict was read out.

On the charge of shooting the RAF pilot: *guilty.*

On the charge of the Russian atrocity:- *not guilty.*

He betrayed no reaction as the sentence of death by firing squad was read out, giving only a curt nod to the president of the court.

But when the door of his cell slammed behind him the stiff, military bearing he had maintained throughout the trial left him, and he slumped on to his bed.

The only thing that had given him any comfort and satisfaction were the words of an Allied officer giving background information on his behalf.

He said the fighting had been some of the most savage and bloody of the war, the attrition rate in both armies higher than anything on the Eastern front. There had been shootings of prisoners by both sides.

The Germans in Normandy had been vastly outnumbered, yet had fought with great bravery, and the SS were the bravest of the brave.

Not for the first time he regretted not pulling the trigger when he'd had the chance.

And he still had no news of the fate of Inge. If she were dead then at least they would be together again when his time came.

If she was still alive his heart ached to see her one last time on this earth before he went to his maker.

And to see his son – or daughter. He must be a father by now.

While his defending counsel lodged an appeal, Walter asked the officer in charge of the prison if it would be possible to try and trace her. He had last heard of her being in Berlin when the Russians had taken the city, and he had heard nothing since.

The formally correct colonel said he would see what could be done.

Walter was reading Proust when the cell door clanked open and the captain appeared, excited by the news that the American witness had come forward. He couldn't travel, but a letter was being sent to the court.

Consequently the date for his execution had been put off for a month.

Two weeks later he was returned to the dock.

The letter was read out by the captain. It stated that he, one Second Lieutenant John Fairfax, had been a prisoner of the defendant when they had come across a mortally wounded German on the date entered into the court records.

In his opinion Walter Raus had acted mercifully, and had certainly not been involved in shooting any Allied prisoner on the day in question, a day in fact, in which he had behaved impeccably to him, his actions saving his life.

The death penalty was commuted to life imprisonment, to be served in a German prison in the British zone.

Before he was moved, together with twenty other prisoners, the officer in charge came to see him, courteous, but formally correct as always.

They had found Inge, alive and well, still living in Berlin.

The Commandant held out his hand. There was a letter in it.

Left on his own, Walter looked at it for a long time before he opened it, and began to read.

*My darling husband*

*Writing to you is a miracle come true. I thought you were dead, and I am led to believe we have found each other again – just as we might have been parted for ever in the most cruel of circumstances.*

*Thank God I did not know, but we do not get any information in this camp, though they look after us very well.*

*I cannot express in words my joy and my renewed faith in Almighty God. But there is one sad thing I must tell you straight away. I'm afraid our dear son – yes, a son, I called him Gerd after your father, died at birth. He was a fine-looking boy. They said that in other times he would have survived, but I think God was kind to us. Terrible things happened after the Russians came.*

She said no more, but he realized what was left unsaid.

The calm, stoic face of a German officer, for whom death held no fear, which had been present throughout his trial was no more.

Head bowed, the tears slowly trickled down his face.

Three years later, dressed in an old civilian overcoat and trilby hat, carrying a brown-paper parcel done up with string – his worldly possessions – Walter Raus shook hands with the sergeant at the pedestrians door of the huge prison gate. He stepped out, blinking in the weak sunshine, on to a cobbled street surrounded by bombed-out ruins.

Inge was waiting, across the road, dressed in a headscarf and a shabby raincoat tied by the belt at the waist.

They stood looking at each other for quite a while before he crossed the road, waiting as a tram rattled past, and came up to her.

They searched each other's eyes, said nothing as she threaded her arm through his, and began to walk away from the bleak, towering walls.

The war for Walter and Inge was at last over.

# CHAPTER FIFTY-ONE

Maddie was sitting out on the terrace; if the weather permitted she always liked her breakfast outside.

She finished drinking her fresh orange juice as Mr Godfrey, in his always-immaculate short white coat and pin-striped trousers, brought a rack of toast and set it down on the glass top of the wrought-iron table.

'Thank you, George.'

He picked up the coffee pot and poured the dark liquid into the white interior of the porcelain cup.

She was playing that night, so she was having a cooked breakfast: her 'pre-ops' breakfast, as she liked to call it.

After that she would go to her piano on the first floor of the Regency house, and spend an hour refreshing her memory of the way she liked to interpret certain passages of the work. Then, after a light luncheon she would be driven by him to the afternoon rehearsal with the full orchestra. She would not eat again until the performance was over. That night she was at the Royal Albert Hall, in a concert that was part of the Proms season.

She was to play one of the romantic piano concerts on which she had built her reputation, and it never failed to remind her of the past – of the war.

Maddie read her newspaper as she bit sedately into a slice of toast.

She wondered frequently these days what had happened to that bright new world they had been expecting all those years ago when the war should at last be over?

The headline today was about another bomb outrage, and inside there was a big report on children taking drugs – *children* for God's sake. Sadly Maddie shook her head.

It was a different world from the one she had grown up in, but she was nearing sixty; perhaps she was just getting to be a cranky old woman.

She finished her breakfast, and wandered up to the music room, stopping on the way in the elegant hall with its black-and-white marbled floor, to smell the roses on a polished sidetable.

Maddie practised for over an hour on her white Steinway that stood in the corner of the parquet-floored room, with one of its walls lined with scores and books devoted to music.

At last, satisfied, she went across the landing to the small room that Edna, her diary secretary and general factotum, occupied.

Edna looked up, pressing a finger to the middle of her rather old-fashioned glasses, pushing them back on to her nose.

'Good morning, Madam.'

'Morning, Edna. Any problems?'

Edna picked up a fax sheet.

'The organizers of the Lucerne Music Festival wondered whether you would mind changing from the Tuesday to the Wednesday. It's to do with the opening ceremony going on longer than expected.'

Maddie frowned. 'Can we?'

Edna turned the pages of a large desk diary.

'Yes, but it would mean you travelling back that night. There is a flight at 11.45 – gets in at Heathrow at ten to one.'

Maddie put a finger and thumb to her chin, pinched some flesh and thought for a moment.

'Well, it's not ideal, I agree, but I've got the rest of the week off – right?'

Edna nodded.

Maddie sighed. 'All right, tell them that will be fine.'

She shook her head.

'I think I might start easing back next year.'

Edna said nothing. She'd heard that said before, last year – and the year before.

'Right, if that's all, I'm going to take Trixie for a walk around the park before lunch.'

Maddie got to the door before Edna said: 'Oh, there was a phone call – from the MOD of all people.'

Frowning, Maddie asked: 'What did they want?'

Over the years she had always obliged the forces in any way she could, usually with fund-raisers for SSAFA rather than entertaining the troops – she smiled to herself: there wasn't much call for a concert pianist with the rank and file.

'They didn't really say, just that they would like to speak to you in person. I didn't disturb you at rehearsal, and rather than have them calling again, I took their number.'

Maddie looked bemused.

'The MOD? That's unusual.'

Edna's eyes twinkled behind the glasses.

'It sounds like a really big favour; maybe it's that all-star command performance we've heard about.'

Smiling, Maddie pulled a face. 'Unlikely. Anyway, would you ring them? I'll take it in my bedroom. Give me five minutes.'

'Very well.'

Maddie climbed the stairs to the second floor and entered the wide room with its two floor-to-ceiling windows. It was bright and airy, with a large double bed facing a white marble fireplace.

Maddie finished refreshing her make-up and was regarding herself in the brightly lit wall mirror when the phone rang.

She slipped into the bureau chair and picked up the heavy, 1940s receiver.

'Hello.'

Edna's voice came over the line.

'I've got a Squadron Leader Howard on the phone for you. Still wouldn't tell me what it's all about.'

'Very well.'

There was a click and then a man's voice said:

'Dame Madeleine?'

'Speaking.'

There was a slight pause, before he said: 'My name is Howard. I have some rather personal news for you. Do you wish me to continue, or I could of course come round and see you, at your convenience.'

Mystified, she frowned and said: 'Of course, continue, though I don't understand . . . personal?'

Howard cleared his throat. 'Yes. I work for the Royal Air Force Central Casualty Section. We've been in communication with the French Air Force. They had notified us that marshland being drained for development had revealed the crash site of an RAF aircraft – a Typhoon.

'It was in deep but parts have been incredibly well preserved in heavy clay and pockets of high-octane fuel.'

She listened, finding it increasingly difficult to breathe, as he continued: 'The subsequent excavation by a specialist team has left no doubt. . . .'

Maddie closed her eyes, swayed in the chair, and would have collapsed if she had been standing.

She interrupted him.

'It's Flight Lieutenant Cochran's plane, isn't it?'

There was a slight pause, before he answered quietly:

'Yes.'

In 1953, accompanied by her little daughter, Dawn, she had attended the inauguration by Her Majesty the Queen, of the memorial to the missing, at Runnymede.

The names of 20,466 airmen of the British, Commonwealth and Empire were commemorated. They had no known graves.

Maddie refocused, came back to the present and said sharply:

'How do you know – how can you be sure it's his?'

'The serial number of the aircraft tallies with the records, and besides . . .' his voice tailed off.

Maddie's heart quickened. 'There is something else?'

'Personal effects have been recovered, identification discs and so forth, and' – he paused again, eventually saying gently – 'some remains.'

Edna was writing when the housekeeper, Mrs Godfrey, put her head around the door, looking worried.

'What is it, Mary?'

Mrs Godfrey came further into the room.

'Miss Cochran,' she still wasn't used to calling her employer 'Dame Madeleine', 'is everything all right?'

'Why do you ask?'

'Well, I've been up to her room with fresh towels, but I could hear her crying so I didn't knock.'

Edna frowned.

'Well, she was all right ten minutes ago. Oh, I wonder . . .'

'What?'

'I've just put a call through to her from the MOD, a squadron leader, he said it was personal when I enquired what it was about.'

Mrs Godfrey looked at her with growing concern.

As the two women stood outside Maddie's door Edna hesitantly gave a knock. 'Dame Madeleine?'

There was no reply. She did it again, but this time Mrs Godfrey suddenly opened the door a little and called out: 'Miss Cochran, are you all right?'

Maddie's small voice carried to them: 'Come in.'

She was lying on her bed, a handkerchief in one hand, her eyes red and puffy. In her other hand was a photograph that she always kept on her bedside table. Both the women knew it very well.

She looked at them and fought back a sob.

'It's Robbie, they've found him.'

Despite all the entreaties of the household and her agent, whom they had contacted, Maddie was adamant. She was going to drive to Little Staughton; she had a sudden, desperate urge to be where they had first set eyes on each other.

'But Maddie, you might not be back in time, and the rehearsal. . . .'

She closed the car door on her agent, and then dropped the window.

'Don't worry, I'll see you tonight.'

With that she drove off.

On an overcast afternoon – the sun had clouded over in sympathy with her mood – she found the entrance to the wartime airfield.

There was no longer a guardhouse, but some of the hangars, looking shabby and with peeling paint, were still there.

Other buildings, including the control tower were now surrounded by overgrown nettles and brambles, windows were smashed, ironwork was twisted and rusting.

At last she was there – at the officers' mess where she had first cast eyes on him, upside down, feet on the ceiling.

Except there was no longer a ceiling, no longer a roof, just a concrete floor, pools of water, and an old leather chair, upside down, rusting springs showing through.

But when she closed her eyes she fancied she could hear the boys shouting and laughing, as they had on that fateful night.

Maddie sat for a long time on a lump of concrete, listening to the breeze rustling the long grass, remembering.

Dame Madeleine Cochran walked out with the conductor of the BBC Symphony Orchestra on to the stage of the Royal Albert Hall.

When the applause died away she sat waiting, trembling slightly with emotion, before nodding to the conductor that she was ready.

His baton swung down.

Critics were later to write of the exceptional intensity Dame Madeleine had brought to the piece that night, of a musical experience that had been quite extraordinary in its power and colour, and tender, haunting moments.

For somebody reckoned to be in the twilight of their career, this, they said, was the finest, most moving interpretation that she had ever achieved in the concert hall.

They had not seen the tears falling onto the keys as she had played Greig's Piano Concerto.